A Mind with Wings

A Mind with Wings

The Story of
HENRY DAVID THOREAU

Gerald & Loretta Hausman

Trumpeter
BOSTON 2006

Trumpeter Books
An imprint of
Shambhala Publications, Inc.
Horticultural Hall
300 Massachusetts Avenue
Boston, Massachusetts 02115
www.shambhala.com

9 8 7 6 5 4 3 2 1

First Edition
Printed in the United States of America

⊗ This edition is printed on acid-free paper that meets the
American National Standards Institute z39.48 Standard.
Distributed in the United States by Random House, Inc.,
and in Canada by Random House of Canada Ltd

Designed by Graciela Galup

Library of Congress Cataloging-in-Publication Data
Hausman, Gerald.
A mind with wings: the story of Henry David Thoreau/Gerald and
Loretta Hausman.—1st ed.
p. cm.
Summary: A fictional account of the life of the nineteenth-century
philosopher and nature writer, Henry David Thoreau. Includes
bibliographical references.
ISBN-13 978-1-59030-228-6 (hardcover: alk. paper)
ISBN-10 1-59030-228-1
1. Thoreau, Henry David, 1817–1862—Juvenile fiction.
[1. Thoreau, Henry David, 1817–1862—Fiction.
2. Naturalists—Fiction. 3. Authors, American—Fiction.
4. Concord (Mass.)—History—19th century—Fiction.]
I. Hausman, Loretta. II. Title.
PZ7.H2883MI—2006
[Fic]—dc22
2005018094

He had a mind with wings.
But best of all he had an eye for things.

—*John Ciardi*

To the Reader

HENRY DAVID THOREAU was one of the most influential Americans of the nineteenth century, and perhaps of any century. Boldly and single-handedly, he shaped the environmental movement in America. Parks and public places of natural beauty have flourished because of his passionate advocacy of nature. Thoreau also nurtured the concept of "civil disobedience"—the protest against unjust government. An opponent of slavery, Thoreau later inspired the social action of Mohandas Gandhi and Martin Luther King Jr. You could even say that the seeds of civil rights in this country and beyond—including women's right to vote—were planted by Thoreau.

Henry, as he was called by his friends, is best known for his book *Walden; or, Life in the Woods*, a record of the two years and two months he spent living simply and in harmony with nature at Walden Pond in Concord,

Massachusetts. This book is widely considered one of the most influential and compelling works of American literature. Yet, we have often wondered, who was the living man who gave us *Walden*? Where do we find him walking, talking, scratching, and joking with his friends?

As it turns out, Henry kept personal notebooks throughout his life, where he wrote his observations about nature and the people he met and talked with on his daily walks: farmers, fishermen, laborers, loafers, and close friends. In our opinion, these notebooks contain some of his best and most endearing writing, and so we've drawn on his private notebooks in creating this narrative of his life.

The living, breathing Henry can also be seen in a number of good biographies, and we used them in preparing *A Mind with Wings*. In particular, *The Days of Henry Thoreau* by Walter Harding and *Henry Thoreau: A Life of the Mind* by Robert D. Richardson Jr. yielded unusual facts about the young Henry Thoreau.

For firsthand observations of the man, we turned to *Thoreau: The Poet Naturalist* by Ellery Channing, Henry's best friend. We also studied four of the books written by F. B. Sanborn, another contemporary. Lastly, we used *Henry Thoreau as Remembered by a Young Friend* by Edward Waldo Emerson, son of Henry's mentor Ralph Waldo Emerson. These works were written in the style of the times, and they contained remembered phrases of Thoreau's, which we did not have to alter very much, and perhaps only shortened on occasion.

Perhaps the most important book of all, for us, was *Men of Concord*, edited by F. H. Allen and illustrated by N. C. Wyeth. This volume (which was made up of excerpts from Thoreau's notebooks) provided the pith and point of Henry's being as a naturalist and as a man. Here he appears as a jokester, wordsmith, and keen observer all at the same time. Mainly, though, it's possible to see Henry as a fun person, a man of many moods whose chief amusement is laughing without moving his mouth.

Our dialogue is crafted out of Henry's own statements. Henry's answers to the questions that were raised in his lifetime gave us plenty of good material. He was asked a great many questions, and he answered all of them. Sometimes Henry's poetry provided answers that were not available elsewhere, so we used his verses too.

We hope we have provided a snapshot of a man who was simple, unpretending, and mostly quiet—unless he was singing and dancing and clicking his heels for children. A man of serenity—except when roused to perform a selfless act, such as being jailed for protesting unjust laws. A man of maturity—except when he was being silly. Henry was always mindful that the road was wide and many people were walking on it. He loved everyone and everything—except injustice.

He measured things up in his notebooks, said what he had to say to make the world a better place. In a sense, Henry Thoreau had a twenty-first-century mind in a nineteenth-century world where slavery was still legal. If we have briefly captured—but not trapped—this Thoreau, then all the better, because he has so much to say about today, and we need to listen to him.

Gerald and Loretta Hausman

A Mind with Wings

The Name

HENRY THOREAU WAS BORN in July on his grandmother's farm in Concord, Massachusetts, in the year 1817. Six weeks later, he was christened David Henry after his paternal uncle, who had just died of tuberculosis at the age of twenty-three. So Henry got a good name, but given time, he changed it. His whole life Henry Thoreau did things like that, turned things over to his liking. Turned them around—like changing his name from David Henry to Henry David. Turned them upside down and inside out. He got a reputation for this, too. But his friends called him "the Judge" because he looked so serious. Henry was not like that on the inside, but on the outside he was old even when he was young.

Henry's first experiences may have had something to do with this. Once, when he was fourteen months old, he was playing at the front door of his house and a cow came along and gave him a friendly nudge with her head, which sent Henry sprawling.

A little later, when the family moved to Chelmsford, just down the road from Concord, Henry accidentally chopped off his toe with an ax. He picked up an ax and just let it fall. Off went his toe, rolling like a marble. Henry recovered from that pretty quickly. But a few weeks later he was head-butted by a chicken that knocked him over, which left him chicken-wary for quite some time.

Still, Henry overcame chickens only to discover stairs—down he tumbled, head over heels, knocking himself out at the bottom of the stairwell. It took two pails of water to wake him up.

Henry shared a room with his brother John. They were very different. John slept at night. Henry did not. He shivered all over whenever there was a thunderstorm. When the sky was clear and the stars shone at the window, Henry lay awake and stared at them. His mother found him like that one night, mouth open, eyes wide. Stargazing from his bed.

"Henry, dear, why don't you go to sleep?" she asked.

Henry said, "I'm looking through the stars to see if I can see God behind them."

Why sleep when something so magnificent, so perfectly wonderful, was happening right outside the window of the house? Why does anybody sleep—? Henry asked himself. And with that he closed his eyes and went to sleep.

The Family

HENRY WAS NOT the only one who thought about things in a different way. All the rest of the family were freethinkers, too. He was the third of four children born to John and Cynthia Thoreau. Helen, the eldest, was a shy, bookish, mouse-quiet girl. But like her mother, she thought for herself. No one could take a thought away from Helen, not if she wanted to keep it. And she did, more often than not.

So did John, Henry's older brother. Everyone loved John. More than Henry, maybe. Well, John was more "there" than Henry was, even when they were little children. Yet the two shared a deep love of the woods, and Henry got his passion for bird lore from John, who, almost as soon as he could write, kept a journal.

Sophia was the youngest Thoreau. Like her brothers and sister, she had her passions—for painting and music, particularly. She took after her mother in that she was a real talker.

Henry could speak beautifully—when he wanted to. He was, however, more thoughtful than talkative, and so was John, except John was affable and sociable, where Henry was not—unless of course he wanted to be.

They, the Thoreaus, were all a bit *to themselves*. They had no reason to be—and no reason not to be. They were just that way.

John Thoreau, Henry's father, had been a failure as a teacher and as a storekeeper—but not as a provider. He always kept food on the table. He excelled, finally, at pencil making. This he came by most innocently, and accidentally. John Thoreau's brother, Henry's Uncle Charles, was an avid hiker. One day in Bristol, New Hampshire, he stumbled upon a patch of ground that was chock-full of plumbago, a mineral used for pencil lead. Thus the family fortune was secured, if such could be said of making a modest living in one's pencil factory. Anyway, John and his brother Charles went into the pencil business, the manufacturing and selling of lead pencils to schools, stores, and businesses in and around the Boston area.

Henry, at age five, knew nothing of his father's failures, nor of the lengths he would go to pay off his debts. Once, legend had it, John Thoreau paid a bad mortgage debt with his gold wedding band.

But naturally Henry was unaware of anything except what he felt, smelled, saw, sensed, touched, and dreamed about. He was forever poking into things and thinking about things, and mumbling to himself.

Henry was "Mother Nature's child" before he belonged to anyone else—family included. For if God was behind the stars, Henry decided, he was behind everything. Henry included.

Henry was forever looking under leaves for God—or bugs or anything else. Well, it all came to the same thing for him. Looking was looking and God was God—inside, underneath, behind everything young Henry laid his eyes on.

One day at his grandmother's farm in Concord, Henry saw something that made such an impression on him that it stayed with him for the rest of his life. His grandmother took Henry for a walk through the meadow and into the woods. There in the secret envelope of the hills was a great blue-green pond, set in the darkness of the forest. It astonished Henry that something so grand could be so hidden and yet so available to him once he was there.

The place was so quiet that the screech of a lone jaybird made Henry jump and hold tight to his grandmother's hand. For a long time the two of them stared into the solitude of the place, until it gradually became their friend.

As soon as he could write, Henry picked up one of his father's pencils and put down the name of this magical pond, this "eye in the woods," as he called it.

"Walden Pond," his grandmother had said.

Henry wrote the words and spoke them in his head. They were bright as the sun and dense as shadow, sweet like maidenhair fern and bitter as rotten birch.

In the words *Walden Pond* Henry felt his grandmother's hand, and the big blue eye staring at him, asking, "Who are you?"

The Stick

HENRY LIVED IN A HOUSE that whispered with the petticoats of women. And the women of the Thoreau household—mother, sisters, aunts, and occasionally grandmother—were full of opinions. His mother, Cynthia, spoke out against slavery and founded the Concord Women's Anti-Slavery Society. His three aunts, Maria, Jane, and Elizabeth, left the First Parish Church and formed their own Trinitarian Church. Henry's father, who was no less free-spirited, read to him, taught him to play the flute, and granted him the freedom to roam the woods whenever he wanted to.

At age six Henry had more questions than his schoolteacher, Miss Wheeler, had answers.

"Who owns the land?" he asked one day.

"Why, we do."

Henry asked, "Who is we?"

His teacher frowned. "We, the people," she said.

Henry thought of the muskrat and the chickadee. Were they not people, too? What of the woods? Were the woodchoppers, the hunters and fishers, the barberry pickers and huckleberry gatherers the people? Were there others, unseen? Unknown? What of the people who had followed the rivers and channels of what they called the Musketaquid, now called the Concord River, way before he, Henry, was born? What of the people who were born here before his father's people had ever come from the Isle of Jersey to settle in Massachusetts?

"I found another arrowhead," Henry's brother told him.

"Where?"

"It's up from where we dug mussels, up from the marsh and meadow."

They went there, and found under the squelching, squooshing mud an ancient fire-blackened stone. Then—not one but several—pieces of old charcoal, proof of an Indian campfire.

What of those people?

But he dared not speak too much of his discoveries to Miss Wheeler, who taught her students the glory of the first patriots who rebelled against British rule. That was the fame granted to patriotic Concord, not the ways of Indians who had once lived there.

When Henry misbehaved, which was not too often, Miss Wheeler shut him in the dark attic stairway of the schoolhouse by himself. There Henry was content to hear the sawing of the wind and the battering of the buttonwood trees against the weather-beaten school-house on Walden Street. Sometimes he would sleep out his punishment, just like his Uncle Charles.

It amused Henry to think how often Charles was found sleeping in the summer cellar. Sent down there to nip potato sprouts, Charles usually fell asleep. Henry would find him there dozing—the granite cellar stones sweating in the summer heat, Charles snoring loudly among them.

If Charles woke up suddenly, as was often the case, he would ask of Henry, "Who is your favorite poet?" Or "Why does a woodchuck chuck wood?" Or maybe, "Why do your classmates call you Old Stick?"

To which Henry was quick to cite whatever answer came into his head: "Shakespeare . . . woodchucks don't chuck, beavers do . . . not Old Stick, Odd Stick . . . in the mud, I guess."

Charles added his own opinion that "your brother John is the storyteller, I can see that bright and clear. He takes the whole class at recess and spins yarns for them by the fence. And so what is it you do, Henry?"

"They call me 'the fine scholar with the big nose,' which is all right by me because at least they know well enough to leave me alone."

"One day you won't want them to leave you alone, Old Stick."

"Odd Stick!"

"Yes, Old Stick up the crick—with a scholarly big nose!"

They both laughed.

Walking up the stairs from the cool summer cellar, Henry always felt a little sad. Being underground in the silence of the cellar was somehow as good as it got—a sped-up season. And now they trudged back up into summer, where the air was heavier and the songs of the birds lighter and the daylight lay thick as butter.

Sometimes Henry's love of solitude got him into trouble. Not saying anything made him seem guilty of something he had not done. When a knife was stolen, "Odd Stick did it," someone said.

Miss Wheeler asked Henry, "Well, did you?"

"I did not take it," said Henry.

Finally, when Miss Wheeler found the real culprit, she asked Henry why he didn't say more.

"I knew who took the knife."

Her eyebrows raised. "Then why didn't you say so?"

"I told you the truth. I did not take it."

To Henry, the truth did not belong to anyone. Maybe he learned this from his aunts Maria and Jane. Henry modeled himself after Jane on the outside and Maria on the inside. Maria, all flint and spark, was the talker. Jane, quiet and gentle, kept her observations to herself. But both of them were always true to themselves.

When not in school Henry liked to be in the woods or on the banks of the Concord River. He and John caught an eel there. It whipped around and tried to bite them. Eels have bad tempers; caught eels have worse ones.

Henry said the Indians made cattail pancakes, but the two boys didn't know quite how to make them. They tried to smoke dried pond-lily stems, thinking this was also an ancient Indian practice. When the haze cleared from their heads, the Concord was just as green and lazy as it ever was and the boys knew well enough to leave pond lilies in the water where they belonged.

Henry planted a sprouting potato.

John saw the cute little mound where it was planted, and he dug it up and put the potato in his own garden. Then their big sister dug John's mound up and put the potato in her own garden. Henry saw her do it, and he planted the spud back where it started out in his plot. That sprouting potato provided many more in the fall when he unearthed them and shared his with his family. Henry was more than a little proud of himself. He might be an odd stick, but he was an odd stick with a green thumb.

The River

As HENRY GREW OLDER, people considered him stoic or, at any rate, deadpan. His Aunt Maria said, "I wish he wouldn't walk off all the time." If something displeased him, he went for a walk. This was his way. Once he carried hand-raised chickens to an innkeeper in Concord. Without thinking of the boy's feelings, the innkeeper wrung the chickens' necks in front of him.

"With every wring," Henry told his brother, "I died a little myself."

Surprised, John said, "Did you die a little when I shot that junco so we could see what it looked like up close?"

Henry thought about this, then answered, "That was different."

"How?" John asked.

"It was an experiment."

"Well," said John, "I suppose our innkeeper experiments every time he serves chicken at the inn." John added, "Say, why didn't you just walk off like you usually do?"

"I did," Henry said, pointing to his head, "up here. My feet took a little longer to catch up with me."

Henry liked the boiled chowder the family made from the freshwater mussels and clams they dug out of the Walden sandbar, and he did not mind thinking of how delicious a certain fat woodchuck looked when he saw it in the meadow. "I could almost eat it raw," he said to himself. Was this part of his stoic nature, he wondered? Was he an Algonquin reborn in white skin? Henry was full of contradictions.

At age eleven Henry still wore clothes fashioned from hand-me-downs. Trousers made of his father's old fire bags that still smelled of charcoal no matter how many times they were washed. Henry didn't care, however, as he and John were always up to their elbows in river mud and berry juice.

The river was one of Henry's greatest pleasures. The barges that went up and down the Concord carried loads of brick, iron ore, wheelbarrows, hay forks, and hods of square-headed nails. Sometimes the men on board invited Henry and John to come up and walk the deck. The boys clambered on, barefoot and grinning.

How buoyant they felt suspended above the water that passed under them and how lovely to feel the flutter of wind and to see the sudden dive of a hawk over the downs. And how strange, Henry thought, to see the somber houses of Concord all lined up in a row and rooted to the ground. They seemed sad compared with the free-floating, independent barges. In Henry's mind the river and its crafts knew things that the Concord clapboards did not.

"Why don't you build your own boat?" Uncle Charles said to Henry one summer day in 1833, when Henry was sixteen.

There was no need to think twice; Henry did what Charles suggested. He and John built their first wooden boat, *The Rover*. It took them no time at all using borrowed wood, old forgotten wood stacked up in a shed behind their house, and, of course, some prime timber their father kindly yielded for the project.

The hours they idled on Walden Pond no one— least of all the boys—could have accounted for. Often Henry went out alone. Lying on his back looking up at the clouds, he let *The Rover* go where she would. Drifting, wind-willed, Henry dreamed with his eyes wide open.

"Idleness is not bad," he remarked to John one afternoon.

John smiled. "But is it altogether good?" he asked.

"What industry it provides me would fill a book!"

"And if everyone were to be filled with such industry, what would be built, housed, hod carried, hunted?" John said with a sly smile.

"That," Henry answered, "is someone else's industry."

"And yours?"

"—thoughts, my dear brother. Thoughts."

That summer before he went to Harvard College, Henry was already putting his industry to the test by writing his thoughts in a journal. But when he was not doing that, he was trying tricks with his Uncle Charles, who taught him to "swallow his nose."

"Can you also show me how to fall asleep while shaving, Uncle?"

That Charles could not do, but it was something Charles did often enough. Henry would find him seated, hand-mirror on one knee, washbasin on the other, straight razor unopened in his palm. Charles was sound asleep, snoring. His face half-soap, half-stubble.

"Such are the ways of industry," Henry noted.

The University

IT WAS HENRY, NOT JOHN, who went to Harvard. John, being older, was already a pencil salesman for their father's company. Henry, the scholar, certainly fit the bill for university training. But he barely passed the entrance exam, and at the outset, Henry didn't like Harvard any more than Harvard liked him. He had only a little money, and as he put it himself, "I was fitted, or rather made unfit for Harvard . . . mainly by myself." Henry seemed to long for an education of a different order. However, his mother and father wanted him to be a university man, and so off he went.

The first thing Henry noticed was that the college library had forty-one thousand books and the college had only eleven professors. As the professors were often busy and the books were usually idle, Henry delved into them as if they, and not his teachers, were the real instructors. That fall, as the elms were turning gold,

Henry ate at a commons table with five other students. Afterward he went to chapel in a green homespun coat. Straightaway, everyone noticed he was, well, an odd stick. The Harvard dress code called for a black coat. Henry's was greener than the Musketaquid River. His roommate, Charles Stearns Wheeler, who was also from Concord, said to Henry, "They just disciplined that dandy Charles Sumner, did you hear?"

"What for?" Henry inquired, looking up from his book.

"For doing what you're doing."

"Reading?"

"No, silly. Wearing a colored coat. But Charles's was colored plaid, I heard."

Henry grinned. "I've no other," he said plainly. "What about Charles?"

"He's got a trunk full of dress coats. He just wanted to look smart was all."

Henry answered, "We should all be as lucky as the lindens and elms, who drop off their coats of gold as soon as the first crispness comes on."

Charles Wheeler looked at his roommate and scratched his head. "If you say so, Henry."

Even with his coat off, Henry stood, or sat, apart. There was something of the seafarer in his face. He had a ruddy, outdoors look that hid his sometimes sickly physical condition. His face was grave as Caesar's, some said. Others seemed to think he looked Egyptian. No one missed seeing him, yet Henry was almost nowhere to be seen except at the library and at his classes. He liked the small-town atmosphere of Cambridge—the squealing pigs behind University Hall. But still, this was a far cry from home.

When not on the campus, he rambled the hills and hollows just beyond the unpaved streets of the town. There he saw where the squirrels stored their nuts, where the weasels raced across the dry grass, and where the owls coughed up their mouse-bone pellets.

Nature was Henry's other library. He gladly missed out on his friends' drinking sessions and laughing-gas binges on the banks of the Charles River. The sangarees were plentifully poured at Snow's Tavern, and the laughing gas was a science experiment carried on outside of class. "Helps us forget the single cup of tea and the cold rolls at supper every night," Charles Wheeler remarked to Henry when they were studying one night.

Henry poked the fire coals of their small fireplace, and blew on them.

"It's a good thing you're off in the woods so much. If you didn't help yourself to extra wood, we'd freeze in our sleep."

Henry smiled. "Mother Nature provides."

"Yes, but you have to help her," Charles added. "I saw a fellow cut his noon meat ration in half today. Know what he did with it?"

Henry, satisfied the fire was finally alight, shrugged. "No, what?"

Charles guffawed. "He stuck it under the table and

pinned it there with his fork until such time as he could eat it for supper. That way—extra rations!"

Henry gave Charles a quizzical stare. "Extra? I would think it was exactly the same. He merely postponed part of his noon meal until supper."

"He outwitted those idiot proctors. I'll give him that."

Henry said, "He outwitted his belly, that's all."

If Henry's belly growled most of the time from emptiness, he said nothing of it. He and Charles and the other thirty-nine members of the freshman class of 1833 rose a half hour before sunrise and suffered the biting cold when they got dressed. Henry's fires warmed their eyes perhaps a little more than their hands, and then they were off to chapel in the leaf-littered dawn. Breakfast was a cup of coffee and a hot roll, and then it was time to go to class. After classes the boys stoked their fireplace to keep warm. They were allotted six cords of oak firewood, but this was hardly enough, and it represented 10 percent of their yearly school cost. Henry wondered why something given by nature's bounty was so expensive.

The bare room he shared with Charles had no carpeting, a single washbasin, two pine beds, and two desks. There was also a cannonball in each room, which was rolled into the fireplace and heated—a good bed warmer for those who chose to use it that way. But many of the students sent their cannonballs down the stairs as a joke.

The nights and days at Harvard went by more

quickly for some than for others. For Henry, his time away from home was filled with quiet longing. He dreamed of Concord, his brother John, his parents, his sisters, and his Uncle Charles. He missed his aunts' lively talk. He even missed his mother's monologues. Harvard had none of this familiarity for him. It was hard to make new friends, harder still to make friends with boys who were, some of them, under fifteen years of age. As at Miss Wheeler's infant school and Concord Academy, Henry was the stranger, the odd stick.

On his first trip home to see his family, in October, Henry walked a steady thirty miles to Concord with his roommate, Charles. The last three Henry limped. His feet were badly blistered.

"I'm taking my shoes off," he told Charles.

"It's too cold," Charles replied. "And we still have two more miles to go."

There was no telling Henry what to do. He walked the final miles in his stocking feet, a sight his sisters would never forget. A stockinged boy with a man's will coming home to cold Concord, head down looking for acorns or animal tracks, stumbling sorely as he limped up to the house.

"You're home," his Aunt Jane said to him.

Henry smiled weakly. "The last couple miles from Lincoln to Concord took me three hours."

The Rebellion

IN THE SPRING OF 1834 Henry knew a great deal about
the three Rs of Harvard education. These were, as
Henry wrote home, "rote learning, regimentation, and
rowdyism." It was regimentation plus youth that made
for rowdyism, Henry thought.

He also believed that many of the students at Harvard were really too young to be there. Harvard was like
a glorified academy. Students were expected to memo-
rize vast amounts of text and to be able to provide perfect recitations. All of this amounted to very little
reasoning on the students' part and an effortless com-
mitment on the part of the teacher. It also created a
rebellious spirit among the students.

In the spring of Henry's freshman year a tiny spark
struck the tinder of the student body during a now
famous cross-examination, which triggered the most
violent rebellion in Harvard's history. The Dunkin

Rebellion, as it became known, began one morning when an instructor of Greek named Dunkin ordered a student to recite his lesson. The student fired back, "I do not recognize your authority." This was the first spark of the campus revolution that would soon spread like wildfire.

The student, refusing to recite, stared out the window, as if Dunkin weren't there.

"I said, recite!" Dunkin commanded.

The student continued to look away, as if he couldn't hear Dunkin's voice. Nor could anyone else. Dunkin grew red in the face and stalked off to the office of the college president, Josiah Quincy.

Later that day when the defiant student of Greek was told by Mr. Quincy to apologize to Dunkin, he said he would sooner leave school, and to back up his words, he withdrew from Harvard.

That night, between the hours of ten and one, a nameless and numberless group of students laid siege to Dunkin's classroom. They tore it apart, smashing windows and breaking furniture. After which, exhausted, they went to bed.

The next night guards were up in place to prevent further attacks. But this proved futile. Marauding students made an assault on them. More windows were broken. Rooftops were breached, and oaths of anger were hurled down in darkness. Well-aimed stones drove off the guards, leaving the school in the hands of the students, who soon went once again to bed.

The third morning of the rebellion, the prayers at chapel were disrupted by scraping, whistling, groaning, and all kinds of other noises.

At midnight of the fourth evening, the chapel bell was commandeered and rung without mercy while raging student lions were heard all about the yard. At this point President Quincy threatened a civil tribunal and legal action.

The rebellion continued.

When things were still growing worse, the faculty dismissed the entire sophomore class.

"Where were you, Henry?" asked fellow student John Weiss.

Henry looked neither sheepish nor shallow for having missed the midnight rages. The whole thing had passed him by, but now he was neither thankful nor regretful. As usual, he didn't seem to care one way or the other.

"So, you slipped off into some secret mossy cell?" John suggested.

"I would've, but Charles beat me to it and broke it all apart."

John shook his head. He knew what this meant, and it didn't refer to the Dunkin Rebellion. Charles Wheeler, for no reason, destroyed a nesting family of birds that Henry had been studying for months.

"There's a difference between a bird and a man," Henry said, "which is why birds build their nests so high up. Maybe Harvard ought to consider doing the same with its buildings."

"I suppose I know, then, what you think of this whole thing, the rebellion, I mean. Maybe you think fools rush in where angels are not in the habit of going, is that it?"

Henry stroked his chin. "What fools? What angels? I see only fifteen-year-olds with sticks and stones."

The Woods

HENRY THOUGHT MORE OF CONCORD than of Boston during his Harvard years, which came and went quickly, like spring snow. Before he knew it, he was almost out into the world. And no one so well read was so ill prepared for earning a dollar.

"We graduate on August thirtieth," Charles mentioned one day in July as he and Henry walked along the shores of Flint's Pond, where they were sharing a cabin. "What will you do—after?"

Henry bent down and scooped up a handful of duckweed. "Funny how this stuff blots the pond in the hot days of summer, but when winter comes ice blots out all else."

"Why is that so funny? Seems normal to me," Charles said.

"'Normal is what you see. Extra normal is what you feel.' Mr. Emerson said that."

Charles scratched his head. "How is that an answer to my question, Odd Stick? I'm asking what you're going to do after you graduate."

Henry shrugged. "I could—just stay here."

"Well, you'll get hungry when the pond ice blots out your beloved duckweed. Unless, of course, you harvest and sell the stuff. Hey, Henry, maybe you should try eating some?"

Charles plopped some in Henry's hand.

For a moment, Henry just stared at it, as if he were really going to eat some. Then Charles pushed Henry's hand toward his face and ran off. Henry dropped the duckweed and went after his friend.

"Henry Odd Stick Duckweed, come get your diploma!" Charles tore a piece of white birch bark off a tree and waved it at Henry, who walked steadily up the hill.

When they returned to the cabin they shared, Henry and Charles collapsed on their bunks of straw. Henry let out a heavy sigh.

Listening to Henry wheeze, Charles said, "I guess we shouldn't run so hard. I mean, your lungs and all."

"No, it's all right." Henry always said that when he was short of breath. For the past three years he'd missed weeks, even months, of college classes because of his illness. He suffered from bouts of tuberculosis, or consumption, as it was called. His grandfather had died of it. Everyone in the Thoreau family feared consumption, for it was a killer of young and old, and you never knew when you were going to come down with it.

After a while, Henry answered Charles's question about life after college. "I think what I'm going to do is look at things," he said. "The way we've been doing for the last five weeks out here in the woods."

"There's no living in that," Charles remarked.

"There is—if you're a teacher," Henry said. "But I want to do more than teach. I want to sort my thoughts out and put them on paper. One day, I want to publish them."

Charles threw his feet off his bunk and sat up. "No one makes a living *writing*, Henry."

"Mr. Emerson does."

"He's famous."

"—and, for what?"

"Writing, I guess."

"So it's possible."

Charles spat out the open door of their cabin. "About as possible as walking on duckweed," he said.

The Deacon

WHEN HENRY GRADUATED from college in 1837, he wasn't about to be a minister, a doctor, or even a lawyer.

"I suppose teaching is a family tradition," he told his brother John. Henry's older brother and his sister Helen were both teaching in Taunton, Massachusetts, which was near Concord. Both of them urged Henry to find a teaching job.

Henry accepted the first job that came his way—at the Center School in Concord. This was the same brick schoolhouse that Henry had attended before Concord Academy. Ninety students were enrolled. Fifty-two showed up for classes. They were mostly farm boys and were crowded into a single room, so close that their elbows touched.

At the end of the second week, Deacon Ball, who was a member of the school committee, dropped by to see how the new teacher was doing.

That day there were several distractions. The first was a dogfight outside the brick building. All heads turned to see it. Henry reeled the students back to his lesson. And just at that moment, the deacon strode in. All eyes that weren't on the dogfight were glued on the deacon.

Artfully, Henry reeled all the boys in. But as soon as they were paying attention to him, Deacon Ball left the room without closing the door. Then he called Henry out into the hall.

"Exactly what is it you think you are doing, sir?" the deacon asked.

"Why, teaching," Henry answered.

The deacon's bushy eyebrows raised.

"Teaching, you call it? You know, those ruffians will spoil the school. You've got to discipline them—now!"

"How?" Henry asked.

"Well, you've got to flog them with a stick."

Henry objected. "The Concord school regulations specify that corporal punishment should be excluded 'as much as practical.'"

"Is that so?" Deacon Ball pressed his lips together.

"Yes," Henry said, "it is."

Deacon Ball struck his walking stick on the hard wooden floor. "Then you will have to be thoroughly practical," he said. "Or your students will run right over you."

"I see," said Henry, although he did not.

"Then," said the deacon, narrowing his eyes, "you

do agree to use as much corporal punishment as is necessary?"

"As is necessary," Henry repeated. A small smile crept across his lips.

"Then you will?"

"Well, I won't say that I won't," Henry said.

Deacon Ball drew near. "Say you shall, and I shall go."

Henry was going to say "I shall" to get rid of the boring man. But Deacon Ball turned abruptly and left.

"Thank you," Henry whispered. After that, he went back into the classroom. All fifty-two students were pressed to the windows in a jumble, watching the deacon recede.

For the rest of the afternoon, it was impossible to restore order. Therefore Henry acted upon his contractual agreement and gave several students a whack on the knuckles with his ruler.

"There," Henry said. "I have done my duty."

The duty, such as it was, caused the students to sit down in their seats, hands folded. Three of them, however, stood together and cried.

One boy, Daniel Potter, walked up to Henry and shook a fist at his face. "When I'm grown up I'll whip you for this. . . ."

That night, in the quiet of his attic room, Henry wrote a note. Then he walked out into the crisp fall air and slipped it under Deacon Ball's door.

The note said: "I did what you wanted me to. It

went against my grain. Herewith please accept my resignation."

"You just up and quit?" brother John asked when he returned home.

"I had to," Henry said.

"But Henry, dear," his mother pleaded, "you know that children expect to be punished at school."

"But they don't expect to be punished by one who didn't expect to punish them."

The Pencil

"Henry, you're out of work," Uncle Charles said.

"As if I didn't know, Uncle."

"Well, if I were you, I'd think up something to do," Uncle Charles advised while plucking at his suspenders.

Henry's mother, who was clearing the breakfast table that morning, asked, "Are you going to buckle on your knapsack the way you talked about in college?"

"Seek my fortune?"

"Well, I said then, and I will say it again—I won't have you sitting around here moping," Cynthia said.

"Considering how useless I am to you, maybe I *should* take to the open road."

"No, Henry," his sister Helen said firmly. "Stay with us."

Henry coughed. "If I had no principles, I would have no troubles," he said.

Uncle Charles cleared his throat. "May I say something?"

Everyone nodded.

"Please do," said Cynthia.

"I'm no world winner, Henry. You know that as well as the rest of us. I was born with wandering feet just like you. There's but one cure for that—you either hit the road or you fix the seat of your pants to the seat of your chair."

"Are you saying that Henry should be a road walker or a chair sitter, Charles?" asked Cynthia.

"Neither. I'm saying the boy should make pencils! I stumbled on that plumbago, laid claim to it. Look at it now. My brother John's done right well by it. So, now it's Henry's turn. Let him fiddle with the pencils for a while."

A smile flickered across Henry's lips. "Well, it's gainful work," he said.

"What's more, you can stay at home while doing it," Helen said while drying some spoons.

So it was that Henry Thoreau, the failed public school teacher, turned to pencil making. Henry's father, John, welcomed him into the fold, and Henry went to work as never before. The first thing he did was change the lead that his father was using.

"What's wrong with it?" John Thoreau questioned.

"Nothing."

John stared at him. They were standing in their pencil barn and their fingers were grayish with graphite.

Henry sought his father's eyes. "Well, possibly the lead is too brittle. The point breaks pretty easily, doesn't it?"

John looked annoyed. "Anything else?"

"The lead's too greasy, perhaps."

John Thoreau rubbed his chin. "What else, Henry?"

Henry glanced at his father and went on cautiously. "Well, speaking generally, Father, I don't really favor the way our pencils write."

John Thoreau snorted. Then his eyes glittered with wry humor. "Well, that's quite a pronouncement coming from a famous writer such as yourself. I suppose you don't favor the bayberry and glue I use either."

"Don't know enough about them to criticize," Henry said.

"Well, then, that's the first thing you don't seem to know," John Thoreau said as he wiped the graphite off his hands with his heavily smeared apron.

Two weeks passed. During this time Henry researched pencil making. It wasn't long before he knew more about graphite than his father did. He'd discovered that the reason Gorman pencils, made by Faber & Company, were better than any American brand was a secret ingredient. They mixed Bavarian clay into their graphite.

"Where, oh where, do you expect to find some of that rare glory?" John Thoreau asked when Henry told him the news.

"Right here," Henry answered.

"In Concord?"

"No, in Taunton. There are two companies that use it—New England Glass is one."

John shook his head. "Well, you *are* a funny one, Henry. Where'd you pick up all this information?"

Henry said, "At Harvard library."

His father grinned. "I guess your education is going to pay for itself after all."

"Maybe not just yet, Father. Give me some time."

John Thoreau said he would.

And, in time, Henry refined his father's pencils and made them better. He also created a new grinding mill for the graphite. After a few years of work, there were more pencil-making barns in back of the Thoreaus' house.

However, Henry's health—always precarious—suffered from the graphite dust that aggravated his—and his father's—lungs. Furthermore, every time he held a pencil in his hand, he yearned to write with it. The words in his head were rising up like water behind a dam. One day, he thought, the dam will break. The words will tumble out in a rush. When that happens there won't be enough paper in Massachusetts to put them on.

The Writer

It was Lydian Emerson who answered Henry's tentative knock on the door that cold winter afternoon.

Standing outside, listening to the footfalls that grew louder inside the big white house on Lexington Road, Henry imagined that it was a woman's lighter tread.

Lydian, he thought. Ralph Waldo Emerson's beautiful, kind wife. Henry had met her and Concord's most famous writer once before when a group of college students gathered at the Emerson home for a discussion. Later on, Mr. Emerson helped to sponsor Henry's scholarship at Harvard. So they knew each other slightly.

Then, too, it was Lydian who, in 1838, passed Henry's writing along to her husband. Mr. Emerson was impressed.

"Well, hello, Henry," Lydian said.

Henry was a little shy before Lydian's dark-haired,

regal loveliness. He managed to mutter, "Is Mr. Emerson at home?" Realizing his hands were trembling—and not from the cold—he stuffed them in the pockets of his coat.

"I'll see if Mr. Emerson is through writing for the day," said Lydian as she left the foyer, "but please come in, it's so cold out there."

"I can come back if he's busy," Henry said to her retreating figure. But by then Mr. Emerson emerged from a side door set off from the hall. He was a formal kind of man, always well dressed, and particular about his speech. But he smiled often, and his dignified face was a welcoming one.

"Henry Thoreau?"

"Yes, sir."

Emerson raised his brows. "Oh, no sirs around here, please."

Henry smiled slowly. "All right."

When Mr. Emerson smiled, his eyes shut tight.

"You know," Lydian said in amusement, "you two look a little alike."

Henry chuckled. Mr. Emerson grinned.

Lydian continued. "You both have broad foreheads and blue eyes."

"—and large noses!" Mr. Emerson laughed. Henry laughed with him. From that moment, they were friends.

As time went on, Mr. Emerson and Henry saw more

of each other. They took long walks through the woods of Walden Pond. One spring day while walking, Mr. Emerson was amazed at Henry's familiarity with the woods.

"That common mountain laurel over there," Henry told him, "might crown a young Greek god or goddess, but frankly, I'd rather see it here, unnoticed by anyone but us."

Mr. Emerson paused on the trail and looked about.

"What mountain laurel, Henry?"

"You've never noticed it?"

"Sadly, no. And I've probably walked past it a thousand times."

Henry showed Mr. Emerson the thicket of laurel. The older man looked appreciatively at Henry. He said, "You know these woods like a fox or a bird."

Henry smiled. Then he quoted from one of Mr. Emerson's essays. " 'If life were long enough,' " he said dramatically, " 'among my thousand and one works should be a book of nature. . . . It should contain the natural history of the woods. . . . No bird, no bug, no bud should be forgotten on his day and hour.' "

Mr. Emerson shook his head. "You know my words better than I do. But to tell the truth, this is *your* day and hour, Henry."

"One day," Henry replied, "I'd like to disappear into Walden woods, and not come out."

"You wouldn't be lonely for your fellow man?"

"Am I not my fellow man?"

Mr. Emerson burst out laughing. "Henry," he said, putting his hand on his shoulder, "you do so remind me of myself."

"My pleasure."

"No, mine."

The School

HENRY HAD PROMISED HIMSELF not to teach again. But thanks to Mr. Emerson, he went back on his promise. In June 1838, Henry opened his own school, in his own home. And by the end of the month, he had four boys from Boston, all of whom boarded with the Thoreaus.

That same summer the teacher at Concord Academy resigned. Thus Henry rented the old schoolhouse for five dollars per quarter, and his new Concord Academy began as a preparatory school that charged six dollars per student per quarter and had enough students signed up to warrant another teacher. Henry asked his brother John to join him. John agreed, and before long the brothers Thoreau had twenty-five students, the maximum number they could handle.

In the evenings Henry glowed when he talked about

his favorite students. "I like the Alcotts," he told John, "especially Louisa May."

"What do you think of Edmund Sewall?"

"I've taken him sailing on the Concord River and hiking to Walden Pond. It's impossible not to love him."

"Yes, I feel the same way myself. Such a good and gentle boy. Did you know, Henry, his pretty sister Ellen is coming to visit? Do you remember when we first met her?"

Henry nodded. "Yes. Edmund said Ellen was coming. Where will she stay?"

"Why, here, I believe," said John.

"Think of it—a female version of Edmund," said Henry.

"Yes," answered John. "I think of it a great deal."

Concord Academy began classes at eight thirty. Henry started the morning with a little speech that opened with "Have you noticed?" or "Sometimes I have observed . . ." Once he got going, sparks really flew from his tongue. The children loved it. Perched on the edge of their chairs, they listened to every word Henry said.

Assignments were as much projects in feelings as they were lessons in writing.

"I don't think you can write your essays about the seasons this June morning," he told his students, "unless you have something of the seasons in you. Some of you have the noisy wind of autumn blowing through your ears, and you should write of that. Others of you have the chaos of spring, the brooks and freshets roaring in the blood, and you should put pen to paper and say what it feels like to be so disarranged."

"Do you feel a certain season in *you* right now, Mr. Thoreau?" a boy named Thomas asked.

Henry replied, "Well, Thomas, I should say I do. I feel the birds and berries in me most days, even in winter. But now, when I see frogs sitting on their thrones along the banks of the Concord, I set myself up with them—"

Thomas giggled. "You're a frog prince?"

The classroom shook with the students' laughter. Henry cast an eye at his brother John, who, speaking from a chair nearby, remarked, "You got yourself into this, Henry, now let's see if you can get yourself out in time for my solid geometry lesson."

"Well, now that you've all gotten the brash March winds out of your systems, let me say—yes, I *am* the prince of frogs. And a good thing, too. For I know that frogs dream, as do the fishes in the pond and the hawks in the air. Even the grass dreams and the tiny baby buttercups. We're all dreamers of seasons. Each and every one of us."

Henry and John liked to take their students on walks in Walden woods. One day while on one of these educational hikes, Henry bent down and picked up a stone.

"This is not just any stone," he said. "Look at it carefully."

The students studied the green rock, which was covered with a soft coat of moss.

"It's got moss on its back," Edmund Sewall said. "Is that what you wanted us to notice?"

"It's not what I *want*, Edmund, it's what you are *capable of seeing*, by yourself."

However, though they tried hard, none of the students saw much more than a mossy stone. So Henry reached into his coat pocket and brought out his magnifying glass. "Now look," he said.

"Oh, I see it!" Edmund cried. "It's like a little tree all in bloom. What is it?"

"I'd say it's a little tree all in bloom," said Henry, chuckling. "Good work, Edmund."

On another occasion Henry and John took the class down the Concord River by boat. They went past Great Meadows and Ball's Hill, where a small shaded cove beckoned Henry to the shore.

"Do you see anything special here?" Henry asked when the boys and girls were on dry land.

"Good fishing hole," said Martha Hosmer. "My father takes us here."

Henry nodded approval. "Anything else?"

"Good hunting, too," remarked Elijah Wood. "My uncle brings us here every fall."

"Look around. See if you find anything else."

The students spread out, examining everything around them.

Later, when they returned as a group, Henry asked once again what they had seen.

Story Gerrish spoke for all when he said, "We found a freshwater spring!"

"—with sweet water," added Martha Bartlett.

John Thoreau entered into the lesson by saying, "Well, now you know why the Indians camped here and had a village right where we are standing. There was abundant water and fish and animals, and—"

"—and the cove was safe from the wind, which made it easier to do what, Edmund?" Henry asked.

"Sleep at night?" Thomas Hosmer put in.

"Have council fires," added Edmund Sewall.

"That's right," said Henry. "And I'll prove it."

Henry dug into the loamy earth until his shovel rang against a fire-blackened stone. Then another. There was a circle of them.

George Hoar cried out, "Rocks for cooking fires!"

"How do you know?" questioned John Thoreau.

George Hoar looked into the hole Henry had dug. "Well, we can't really know for sure. But when I look at those rocks there, I can just see women bent over them roasting meat or stirring stews."

Henry patted George on the back. "You're a *trainer*," he said.

"All of you are trainers," John added.

The children gloated over this praise, for trainers were soldiers, and soldiers were the bravest and the best.

The Boat

THE STUDENTS LIKED HENRY, but they loved John. John was the more approachable of the two brothers. He was gentle and charming, and he reached out to his students in a way that Henry could not. John was just as well-read as Henry, but he did not use his knowledge in the same way. Perhaps John was born to be a teacher, while Henry was born to teach. There was that difference between them, and the children felt it.

In any event, the students played little jokes on Henry because of the formal way he presented himself. Walking in the woods, Henry was the odd stick he'd always been.

On a bird walk, one of the student's drew a good likeness of Henry as a heron. He was drawn as all nose, or as the students said, all beak. Viewing the work of art, Henry commented with a smile, "Is that an egret or a heron? They're not the same." He could take pokes as well as the next person, but it didn't make him any less reserved. His seriousness about learning was an essential part of his nature.

Once when Henry was walking to school in the morning, George Hoar cut the bell rope in the schoolhouse. Another boy climbed into the bell tower and frantically rang the bell.

Henry and John heard the commotion, gave one another a puzzled look, and shrugged. Neither made a fuss over it. Ropes and bells and silly boys didn't bother them as long as the boys did their homework. Henry and John put up with a lot. However, when the young boarders tipped over a bowl of Mrs. Thoreau's pudding one night, they were given salt fish for supper.

Normally the students ate very well, however. Mrs. Thoreau's bread was wonderful. So were her pies. As a rule the boarders got used to vegetables and fruit, with little or no meat, because the Thoreaus grew much of their own food. Henry's homegrown melons were famous in Concord, both for their size and for their color. The whole family loved fruit and ate a lot of it when it was in season. So did their boarders.

Sometimes Henry and John wanted to be off by themselves, as they had always done when they were boys. They often spoke about going on a trip together.

"I dreamed of an unhurried boat trip down the Concord and Merrimack," John announced at breakfast one summer morning.

"Yes," said Henry, "and we're almost done with the new boat. Why not add a few things for extra comfort, and follow your dream?"

"What things?" John wanted to know.

Henry, always the inventor, revealed his plan for a set of wheels.

"Wheels on a boat? Henry, even for you, that's a bit of a stretch."

However, when John saw that Henry was perfectly serious, he added, "Well, brother, shall we push it or float it?"

Unruffled, Henry replied, "The wheels are for mounting the boat on dry land when we come to a waterfall. We'll simply set her up and push her along until we come to a deep enough spot to launch her."

John shook his head. "Why should I be surprised, Henry? You always were the thinker."

So they built wheels for their boat, which was shaped like a fisherman's dory. They named her *Musketaquid*, the Algonquian name for the Concord River, which meant "grass-ground river." After furnishing oars, masts, sails, and poles, the brothers were ready for their trip.

"What will we do when it rains?" Henry asked John when everything was laid out for the trip.

"We'll have to secure some sort of lodging," John answered.

"Not if we have a tent. That'll give us shelter for the night. One of the masts can be used for a tent pole."

John nodded. They brought along a buffalo hide for

warmth, and a few of Mrs. Thoreau's rhubarb pies, and then they were ready to launch their boat. Family and friends waved as the two sailed smoothly round the bend.

Concord slipped away.

Henry and John were finally on their own.

That first night out, they set up camp and ate one of the big melons from their garden and a piece of Mrs. Thoreau's bread dipped in hot cocoa.

Henry spotted a fox stepping delicately past their campsite and noted it in his journal.

Then, way off in the far hills of Lowell, a blossom of flame rose up on the horizon. Henry and John lay on the grass, watching and listening.

"Here we are," Henry said, "at perfect peace with the world. Yet off in those hills to the south, there's a terrible thing happening—a fire."

"From here," said John, "it's almost a pretty sight. The distant bells, the faint firelight on the night sky."

"I bet our friend the fox sees it, too."

John rolled on his side. He faced his brother in the gathering darkness.

"How do you know that, Henry? Do you know where the fox lives? Did you see its burrow?"

Henry chuckled. "I like to think that the creatures are just like us, John. The muskrat we saw earlier, well, he chooses a house with an open tunnel that has the best view of the river. The fox has artistic taste, too, I think. What's better than a blueberry terrace carved out of the hillside so he can view the far-off comings and goings of men? High enough to see everything. But low enough to get down to the riverbank in a hurry. I believe the muskrat and the fox have art sense as well as survival sense."

John considered this. Lying in the dark, he smiled.

"Well, Henry, if you say so. As for me, I have just enough art and survival sense to fall asleep." And with that, John closed his eyes and slept.

Not Henry. He was thinking about the beautiful face of Ellen Sewall, sister of his student Edmund. She'd been at the dock to see them off. Henry couldn't shake the feeling that Ellen liked him.

Or was it John that she liked? Henry wasn't quite sure. He wanted to be, but he couldn't be.

All he knew was that he might be in love with Ellen. Might be, he told himself. Then he, too, smiled and slept.

All during that week, while taking up the wind in their sails and moving along in the *Musketaquid*, Henry thought about Ellen. He couldn't get her face out of his mind. Her shining dark hair and the way it framed her light, sparkling eyes. The lines of her face were serene, he thought. Smooth and honest and lovely to look at.

One night when the stars were so bright they seemed to pierce through the roof of their tent, Henry composed some lines in the golden glow of the lantern. Those ice-pointed stars made him think of winter weather. In the midst of summer, he thought of ice, and in his poet's mind, two seasons merged into one. Wintersummer.

Was he just a winter boy? he wondered. A boy so cold and aloof he carried the northern rivers in his veins even when summer was at hand? Was he really in love with Ellen, that pretty summer girl, whose warmth was like the lantern light beckoning the moths? Henry didn't know. His pen scratched on, but he really didn't know. Whatever he was writing, it was for Ellen. Of that he was sure.

For a long time Henry penned verses while he listened to his brother breathing. John sounded like a raspy saw. Henry guessed that John was probably just as much in love with Ellen as he was.

At last Henry put down his pen. He watched two dusty moths circle the globe of gold.

If John was in love with Ellen, what was Henry going to do?

The Moon

"WHAT'S GOTTEN INTO YOU?" John asked Henry. The brothers were weeding the family garden one week after their trip.

After a little silence, Henry said, "Well, I guess there's no remedy for love—but to love more."

John grinned. "And what is it you love now, Henry? I imagined you were in love with the sunrise this morning, the way you looked at it so fondly. Or is there something else that holds your affection right now?"

Henry sighed. "I fear it might be something else," he said.

The sun was strong, and the shadows of the afternoon were long. At the edge of the garden the black-eyed Susans towered over Henry's head, nodding in the wind off the Concord.

"I'm afraid it's much the same with me," John explained ruefully.

Henry knew what John meant without his brother's saying any more about it.

Ellen. She was the only flower in the garden right now.

They feared to bring up her name, knowing that what would hurt the one would wound the other.

When Ellen did come to the Thoreau house to stay with the family, she saw two brothers with good intentions fussing over her. Perhaps no one else noticed—perhaps everyone did, including Ellen. But the brothers did not speak of their feelings to one another. That was their pact; they felt much and spoke little.

However, it was John who finally left subtlety behind. He made a brave move forward and met Ellen a little more than halfway.

Henry, seeing John step ahead of him, held back. His own feelings were so bottled up by now that it was almost a relief to let his brother go where he feared to go himself.

I have everything to lose, he told himself, if I do either one or the other. If I go after her, I will hurt John's feelings, and maybe ruin his chances. If I hold back, I ruin my chances, and maybe hurt Ellen's as well. If only I knew how she felt, I could do the right thing for everyone.

But he didn't know.

And Ellen didn't tell. Not right away, anyway.

Time passed. Ellen stayed right on living with the Thoreaus. Between berrying and boating, she saw a lot of John and more than a little of Henry, who hung nearby in spite of himself. To her father back in Scituate, Massachusetts, Ellen wrote, "I cannot tell you half of what I have enjoyed here."

By that, did she mean that half of her heart went to Henry and the other half to John? She liked them both equally, she thought. But, being a proper New England woman, she rarely showed her affections.

In Ellen's mind, Henry was all poetry and poverty. John, who was just as impractical, was at least more worldly than Henry, but both brothers were transcendentalists, and this was something that was alarming to Ellen's parents. The Sewalls were conservative Unitarians.

Transcendentalists, as far as the Sewalls were concerned, were nothing more than pantheists. That is, they were people without a formal religion who worshipped trees and flowers. They were godless and churchless nature lovers. In short, rebels and heathens. That is what the Sewalls thought, anyway. Nothing could have been further from the truth. Henry and John were, in fact, transcendentalists, but they believed strongly in God. They just thought, as did many other members of their group, that God was in all things, and you didn't need a church to feel his presence. You could feel it on a walk in the woods.

Well, the Sewalls had other ideas for their daughter's future. The Thoreaus were no match for Ellen. They were poor, empty-pocketed schoolteachers. She was bred for better things, they told her.

Still, the three were often seen in Concord walking and whispering, talking and sharing. When Ellen left for home, she boarded the stagecoach in tears. Truly, she was quite helpless to choose between Henry and John. Deep down, she loved them both.

And so she gave her heart to neither.

In her absence, after she'd gone home to Scituate, Henry sent Ellen poems.

She received them gladly, but for some reason, she forgot to thank him. Henry suffered over this, but he suffered secretly, as he did with everything that meant a lot to him.

John, seeing Henry withdraw into himself, stepped forward again. This time he boldly asked Ellen to marry him.

Surprisingly—even to herself—Ellen accepted, then refused. No doubt Ellen was, at this point, very confused.

Henry, speaking in code, wrote in his journal—*How many Persias have been lost and won . . . ? Night is spangled with fresh stars.* By which he meant, "In two days my brother has come and gone. Now I know the answer is no. For me the sky again is clear."

"I fear," John told Henry when he returned from Scituate, "that your cause has gone down with mine."

"How?" Henry asked.

"Well, it's not you—or me—she'll have, brother. She'll have neither of us."

Henry's face looked blank. "But why?"

John, having just returned from Scituate, knew all too well what Ellen was up against at home. He'd met Ellen's stern father and strict mother. At last he said to Henry, "You see, the old man has no interest in dreamers . . . of the transcendental type." He tried to chuckle over this, but he failed to do so. He smiled instead.

Henry knew that smile. It was his own.

"Is *that* what he calls us—transcendentalists?" Henry never liked labels.

John said, "Yes, we're Mr. Emerson's boys, he says. You know, men without a church. He told me, straight off, 'Your faith is the open woods. Mine is under a white steeple.'"

"Did you say anything back to him?" Henry questioned.

"Well, I might've said, 'Our purses are empty but our hearts are full.' He'll have none of us, no matter what you or I say. We're not much of a catch, Henry." This time John laughed and Henry joined him.

"I guess you've got that right," Henry said.

That night Henry tossed and turned in his bed. Finally he got up and wrote by candlelight. In his journal he expressed the idea that his real true love was nature. But somehow, after writing this, he then wrote Ellen a letter with a standard proposal of marriage. The following day he put it in the mail. "There," he said, "that's done."

A few weeks passed.

Henry suffered terribly. The hours went by very slowly.

If Henry looked bad, John looked worse.

Both of them were lovesick.

And then the letter came. Henry opened it. Then he walked out to where John was working in the garden. "She's turned down her second Thoreau," he said. John, bent over a patch of turnips, lowered his head. "She'll not regret it," he said.

"No, I don't think she will."

In truth, Ellen was still embarrassed over changing her mind about John. Now she'd rejected Henry. But whatever she felt—and it was a burden to her—she heard her parents loud and clear. No more Thoreaus.

Unlike John, Henry took his refusal in stride. At least on the surface he did. In his journal he noted how it was to fall in love with the "cold cold moon." If he wept over his first love, it was in the attic bedroom, where he shared his feelings with the rafters, the tree at his window, and his beloved journal. In spite of his disappointment, his spirit was buoyant. Henry told John, "To have known love is as good as having it."

John said, "Is it really, Henry?"

The Nanny

CONCORD ACADEMY lasted only three years. Partly this was because John Thoreau's tubercular condition worsened and he couldn't work anymore. Henry, unwilling to run the school by himself, closed the door to Concord Academy in 1841. And now he needed a job.

He found one as a handyman at the home of his friend Ralph Waldo Emerson. Lydian Emerson saw Henry's talents right away. "You can plant a garden, graft an apple tree, mend a fence, and clean out a clogged chimney. Is there anything you can't do?"

"Well, I can't go about the country and lecture like your husband does," Henry answered.

"Maybe, in time, you will," she said wisely.

When he wasn't mending things for Lydian or helping his father make pencils, Henry loved to take four-year-old Waldo Emerson on nature walks. Sometimes he stood in the Emersons' hall with his flute. Blowing a note, he summoned the Emerson children to a special fireside storytelling.

Waldo admired Henry's seafaring face, his gray-blue eyes that were both serious and sad. His sister Ellen adored Henry, too.

Once, Henry took Waldo down to the Concord to look at, well, anything that came along. Soon they saw two turtles sunning themselves on a log.

"What are they doing?" Waldo asked.

"*Doing?*" Henry said in surprise. "Why, they *do* whatever they like. After all, they've got no employers trying to boost their productivity."

Later, when Waldo was watching a battle of red and black ants, Henry said, "Somewhere in the midst of those tiny bodies is a warrior Achilles."

Waldo knew about Achilles, the legendary Greek soldier of the Trojan War, the hero of Homer's *Iliad*. Henry had told Waldo all about ancient Greece.

"I don't see Achilles, Henry," Waldo said, bending closer to the ground.

"Look for Hector, then. Or better yet, Helen of Troy."

Being with Henry, it never occurred to Waldo that ants weren't just like humans. Nor, for that matter, that humans weren't sometimes just like ants.

"We share our weaknesses and our strengths with them, Waldo, our largeness and our smallness," Henry explained. "What is the fate of an ant to a man? What is the fate of a human to an ant? And yet, if you look at those clashing red and black creatures, you will see a drama no different from our own."

"But why do ants and people want to fight?" Waldo asked.

"That is the question of the ages, Waldo. And we won't be able to solve it today." Henry's face brightened. "'Tis merry," he cried, "'tis merry in the good green wood—" and with that, he spun a tale of Robin Hood and Sherwood Forest, and Waldo forgot all about the Homeric battles of ants and men.

The Fever

THE NEWS THAT HIS BROTHER was seriously ill reached Henry a few days after John's accident.

"Tell me what you did, how it happened," Henry asked John, who was already bedridden with a high fever when Henry got to the Thoreau house.

"I couldn't have seen it coming," John said with a small shrug. "So small a thing." John held up his bandaged finger so Henry could see how minor the injury really was. John was almost apologetic about it.

Henry drew a chair up close to the head of the bed.

John remarked, "—*'tis not so deep as a well, nor so wide as a church-door.*"

"*But 'tis enough,*" Henry said, finishing the phrase.

John smiled. "You remember your Shakespeare."

Henry clicked his tongue. "One doesn't forget *Romeo and Juliet.*" Then he frowned hard at John and added, "Nor does one forget how to shave . . . . That *is* how this thing happened, isn't it? You cut yourself with your razor?"

"It didn't seem sharp enough to cut my finger, let *alone* my beard," said John. His eyes, though bright with fever, had an impish twinkle.

"You were testing it then?"

John sighed. "Must we talk of this, Henry? I'd sooner hear of your fixing up those chicken feet for Mrs. Emerson. Would you tell me again how you did that, Henry?"

Henry's face relaxed. The worry fled from his eyes. He couldn't refuse John anything, let alone telling him this silly story. He went ahead and told the tale again. "Well, Lydian said their chickens were scratching up the garden, so little Ellen, Waldo, and I caught them, and at my request, Lydian cut the tips off her Moroccan leather gardener's gloves."

John's pale face lit with mirth. "Then what? Tell the rest."

"You know the rest," Henry said.

"But I want to hear it again . . . from your lips."

"Then I shall tell you, although we both know that you know this story by heart."

John's face was damp with sweat, but his blue eyes glittered through the fever. He was impatient to hear of the chickens' new footwear.

Henry continued, as if he were telling it for the first

time. "So, as I say, Lydian cut the tips off the gloves and I tied them on the chickens' feet with string . . . and we outfitted Lydian's hens with little boots."

"Did that stop them from scratching in the garden?" John asked, chuckling.

Henry shook his head. "Not really."

John laughed, coughed, became still. His forehead shone with perspiration. He tried to smile. "I always planned on keeping a stiff upper lip, but now I must do better than that, and keep a stiff upper jaw."

Henry snapped, "You must stop joking about your illness, John."

"I'm *not* joking," John insisted. "If the Heavenly Father gives me a cup, shall I not drink from it?" He gazed out the window.

"Whatever the cup is, you must take it," Henry agreed with a nod.

"Then my cup is . . ." John paused, searching for the right word. "Lockjaw," he said, and slowly turned his face to the wall.

That night a doctor came from Boston and examined John.

Later, Henry saw the doctor's grim expression as he stood in the front hall wrapping a scarf around his neck, preparing to go out into the icy January night.

"Is there no hope?" Henry asked, full of fear.

The doctor didn't flinch. "None," he said. "With tetanus . . . lockjaw . . . there's no cure." With these words, the doctor left the house. Henry found him as cold as the dark winter night. But he understood that the doctor saw too much dying to feel the sorrow of each patient's death.

Henry went back to John's fever room. There he stayed for the rest of the night, sleeping fitfully in a chair. Sometimes his parents, Cynthia and John, came in quietly. They saw the brothers together and, knowing there was nothing to be done, left the room as quietly as they'd come in.

The following day it snowed on and off. By noon John was starting to grow delirious. "I feel I'm going on a short journey," he said to Henry. His drawn thin lips barely parted as he spoke.

"Can't you stay a little longer?" Henry begged.

John, his face burning, eyes glowing, said, "Well . . . to think I almost got married. But then she wouldn't have me."

"Nor me," reminded Henry, but John didn't hear him. He kept coming and going, in and out of consciousness. John's blue eyes, the same color as Henry's, were bright, but the rest of him seemed to be fading fast.

"Will you laugh for me once more, dear Henry?" he said, suddenly waking.

"Yes," Henry promised, "I shall always laugh for you."

Through clenched teeth, John said, "This would've really disappointed Ellen."

"I think she should've married *both* of us," Henry told him.

John murmured something. Henry scraped his chair closer to hear his brother. John said thickly, "We could've all gone out together wearing chicken boots." His eyelids flickered, then shut. He breathed heavily and slept.

Henry wept into his open hand. Outside, the blue sky was absent of clouds. Single snowflakes tumbled down lazily from the sky and tapped against the frost-cornered window. Henry saw them and wiped his tears from his face. What am I doing? he asked himself. He's not gone yet.

The afternoon wore on. The sky grayed, then darkened. The wind bumped the house. John slept. He went from one fever dream to another, murmuring all the while. Henry understood little of what his brother said. Finally, exhausted, he drifted off to dreams of his own.

In one he saw himself and John set off on the Musketaquid on that drizzly summer morning. Two brothers, two oars. The earth, the water. Nothing simpler, nor more beautiful. They spoke of postponing the trip because of the rain.

"Should we wait another day?" John wanted to know.

"No," Henry said. "This day is *our* day."

Henry woke and cried again into his hands.

Swiftly a memory came to mind. He and John were picking blueberries at Ball's Hill. Then they were having hot cocoa and fire-warmed bread.

Henry whispered to himself, "Those lazy days on

the river really were all ours. And they will be. Now and forever. Always the oars, beaded with diamonds, rising and falling. Always John's face, smiling."

"We went downriver of a summer's day," he said to his sleeping brother, "and when we returned, it was fall."

Henry went on. "That journey is done. And a new one is begun. But where it leads we do not know."

Suddenly a chilling thought occurred to Henry. What would he do when John was gone? How could his life's journey continue without him? It wasn't death that he feared. But the leaving—John's leaving. Would he ever have a friend like John again?

At that moment Henry's sorrow was so wide he could not see the end of it. His belly was ice. And as the winter day died down, Henry felt his soul die a little with it.

The following day John Thoreau died in Henry's arms.

Two weeks later, tragedy struck a double blow. Little Waldo, the Emerson's five-year-old son, died of scarlet fever.

"If there are any tears left inside me, I will shed them," Henry told his mother. But for the moment, he had no tears. He sat, alone on a gray day toward the end of January, staring at his favorite music box.

Reluctantly, he turned the key. A bright, tinny waltz filled the small room where John had died. Henry looked out the window at the skeletal trees. The gray-barked maples leaning and clicking in the wind. For a brief moment, the bleak look of endless New England winter seemed not to affect him. The music box waltz drowned the dueling of branches by the window. The summery music lifted Henry's heart.

"There is a rotation of the seasons," he said to no one but himself. "A turning of time. The endless course of the river and the wind as they circle and bind the earth; all of this is moving and changing. All of it is in the course of nature. Why should we, as humans, doubt our end as much as we celebrate our beginning? Is there not new leaf even now hiding in the midst of those tight bare branches waving at the window ledge?"

Henry smiled to himself and went on. "There will be much to laugh about, dear John. Why should I ever think that you are gone? When I smile, don't you smile with me? When I talk about chicken boots, aren't you there laughing with me?"

Henry felt a glowing sensation around his heart.

He gazed out the window. Idly picking up one of his father's plumbago pencils, Henry said aloud, "John is still alive. What is the matter with me?"

Then he sat down at his desk and wrote an elegy for little Waldo.

He died as the mist rises from the brook, which the sun will soon dart his ray through. Do not the flowers die every autumn? He had not taken root here.

The Dust

HENRY DREAMED ABOUT JOHN nearly every night. They were in the *Musketaquid* drifting downriver. They were watching a red fox vanish in the goldenrod. They were listening to the song of a hermit thrush deep in the dark pines of Walden wood. John was so alive when Henry had these thoughts of the things they shared.

Once, in a dream, John looked at Henry and said, "I like best the song of the red-eyed vireo, don't you?" Henry was going to reply when he awoke from sleep, feeling certain that John was right there with him.

One night Henry dreamed of John as he lay dying. Henry woke from it feeling sick. He stayed in bed all day. Whenever his mother looked in on him, Henry seemed to have the same death's face that John had when he died. Fearfully, she searched Henry's hands for a razor cut like John's. There wasn't one. Still, she wondered if he was going to live.

For two days the Thoreaus really thought Henry was dying. And it seemed that he was—he ached, he slept, he fevered. He had restless dreams and mumbled in his sleep.

Yet after many days of delirium, Henry snapped out of it.

It took until mid-April for Henry to fully recover from this mystery illness. At last he was able to return to the Emerson house and assume his duties there. But his battles with death had marked him, and his life was not quite the same afterward.

In fact, Henry's spirit was so heavy that Mr. Emerson believed that his friend might be better off somewhere else. Mr. Emerson arranged for Henry to tutor his brother William's children in Staten Island, New York. The opportunities for a young writer were much better in New York City than in Concord. There were, in addition, the greatest libraries and some of the best newspapers.

Mr. Emerson told Henry, "You'll meet Horace Greeley of the *Tribune*, and others, too. My brother and his family will take you in and make you one of them. Bring your journal, Henry, and make contacts in the city."

Henry wholeheartedly accepted this plan. He felt stuck, stagnant. He wasn't ready for the woods—not quite yet. But maybe he *was* ready for the city. Anyway, it was worth a try. So in May 1843, Henry went down to Staten Island, where William Emerson paid him ten dollars and told him to get started tutoring his three children.

A few weeks later, Ralph Waldo Emerson wrote to Henry asking how he was doing.

Henry wrote back, "I haven't set my traps yet, but I'm getting my bait ready."

Mr. Emerson queried, "Does it take so long to bait the traps?"

Henry answered, "My bait doesn't tempt the rats—they're too well fed." What Henry meant, of course, was that his essays were not finding a publisher. The rats, or publishers, were feeding on other writings at the time.

When he wasn't tutoring, Henry visited a number of fine libraries. Amid the many wise volumes and in the pristine sanctity of the great reading rooms, Henry imagined he was back at Harvard, where life had not been quite so difficult for him. He thought dispiritedly, "I am no better off than I was ten years ago. I am still the dreamer without a dream. I still do not know what to do with myself."

After almost seven months of tutoring and reading and making notes in his journal, Henry returned to Concord, no different from when he'd left. It bothered him that the haunted-faced city dweller Edgar Allan Poe was able to get his words published while Henry was not. "He pushes them into crevices I cannot get myself into," he wrote to Emerson. By this he meant that Poe was able to find some curious, narrow places—

magazines and journals—where his writing found an audience.

However depressed Henry felt concerning his failure as a writer, he was overjoyed at seeing the blue Concord sky, which was more welcoming to him now. He told Mr. Emerson, with a sigh of relief, "Once again, I have Concord dust in my boots."

The Friend

BACK HOME ON MAIN STREET, Thoreau shed his city clothes and put on his old comfortable corduroy coat and trousers. His coats and trousers, when he could afford them, were tailored after his own fashion. He was fond of saying, "I must wear them, not the tailor."

Henry's closest friend now was Ellery Channing, the nephew of William Ellery Channing, founder of the Unitarian Church. Sometime in 1840 or 1841, the two men met at Mr. Emerson's, and there was an immediate attraction between them.

Ellery, or C., as Henry depicted him in his journal, was a rebel like Henry, a writer like Henry, and a transcendentalist like Henry. They were so much alike, these two. Channing, however, was married. And there was one other great difference between the two men: Ellery had already done the one thing that Henry said he wanted to do. In 1839 Channing had bravely gone to the Illinois prairie to live in a floorless cabin all by himself. There he farmed, wrote, and contemplated nature. Exactly the thing Henry told Mr. Emerson he wanted to do at Walden.

One clear December afternoon in 1843, Henry was walking toward Concord with that straight, forward-flowing walk that he had, and Ellery, who was also out for a brisk winter stroll, saw him.

"Henry!" he exclaimed, when they were standing in front of each other. "How was New York?"

"Fairly terrible—or terribly fair. One or the other. Whichever, it wasn't for me."

"Did you get to the sea?" Ellery asked.

"Did I get to the sea?" Henry scratched his head. "I got to the sea, but the sea did not get to me—did not get to me *enough*, or I would've stayed."

Ellery grinned with evident pleasure at hearing his friend play with words. "What a charming way to put it."

"Well, you see, whenever I had time to spare I sat for hours in an old ruined fort watching the ships sail up the coast. One day I saw a washed-up horse being eaten by a pack of wild dogs. Another day, I rescued a puppy from that same brutal pack. Sometimes I sat and listened to the song of the seagulls. But nothing was so dear to me as our meadowlark, bluebird, or Concord owl. I liked seeing the island tulip trees, but when I went to sleep, I dreamed of sitting at our back door under my favorite poplar tree."

Ellery listened well. He was as good a listener as he was a talker, and at talking he was a master.

"So, you're home now, Henry," said Ellery. "I've plans for us. I want us to go on a walk from the Berkshires to the Catskills."

Henry replied that he'd love to go on an excursion with Channing, and they left it at that. After saying good-bye, Henry returned to his father's pencil barn. If there was work nowhere else, there were, at least, plenty of pencils, glue, graphite, and clay.

However, the old machine that John Thoreau used to split his wood seemed outdated to Henry. So he went to the drawing board and came up with a new machine. This one drilled a hole into the cedar pencil precisely the size of the lead. Formerly, his father split the wood in two halves and glued it together again. Henry's way was bolder, quicker, and more profitable. Also, by adding more or less clay to the lead, Henry got a harder, or a softer, pencil point.

"You've turned Thoreau pencils into artists' tools, Henry," his father said proudly. His eyes shone with pleasure.

"I hope we sell twice as many," Henry replied, pleased.

They did, too, at seventy-five cents a dozen. And it wasn't long before a great many of them sold in artist supply shops in Boston.

John Thoreau was grateful for the help. Henry was glad he could give it. The two worked well together.

One afternoon in February, Ellery Channing stopped by to see Henry, but John Thoreau didn't want Ellery to see the inside of the pencil barn. What they did in there was a secret. John Thoreau wanted no prying eyes learning his recipes for the perfect pencil. In fact, no Concordian had ever been invited into the barn since the Thoreaus began making pencils there. So Ellery waited for Henry inside the main house. When Henry finally came in, rubbing his hands on a black rag, Ellery whispered, "Your mother talked to me without taking a breath."

Henry said, "Poor thing. The less father listens, the more she speaks. I bet she appreciated your attentive ear."

Ellery gave him a sly smile.

"If I said I liked my dog more than my wife, would you think less of me, Henry?"

"What a thing to say . . . but no," Henry answered. "I think more of most birds than I do of my Concord neighbors, so I'm not surprised at what you say."

"Sometimes I don't like my dog," Ellery confessed with his peculiar little grin. "Sometimes, when I'm all alone, I imagine I've no friends except a few low-lying clouds."

Henry nodded. He knew what that was like.

They were standing in the hall, and Henry beckoned Ellery to sit a spell in the parlor. "No, I feel like walking," Ellery told him.

"Then maybe I'll go along with you and get some of the graphite out of my nostrils."

On down the winter road they walked, murmuring praises of this and that and noticing everything from the crows to last year's frozen hickory nuts still stuck to some branches. After they'd trudged for a while on a thin skin of old, refrozen snow, Ellery asked, "Say, Henry, what's that sticking out of your pocket?"

Henry dipped his hand into his woolen jacket pocket. One by one, he produced some folded papers, pencils, a pocketknife, a spyglass, as well as some stray seeds and a burr he'd just picked up off the ground.

"Have you a new poem?" Ellery asked.

Henry hitched his shoulders. "You mean on this piece of paper? No, this is my indebtedness to my father." Henry held the fluttering ledger sheet out into the weak February sun, and Ellery looked it over.

Dec. 8, 1840—Owe Father	$41.73
Paid, Dec. 17	5.00
Paid, Jan. 1, 1841	15.00
Borrowed, Feb. 2nd	1.35
Paid, Feb. 8th	10.00
Settled debt March 22nd, 1841	

Ellery shook his head. "Why do you carry such old bills around with you, Henry? Do I need to remind you that this is 1843?"

"I know the date, Ellery. But I'm carrying the same

again. I save on paper by borrowing and paying back the same amount."

Ellery chuckled. "Well, don't let me stand in the way of your odd bookkeeping."

Henry didn't. For he knew something that other men of Concord also knew: Ellery Channing frequently forgot to pay his bills. He lived not like the ant but like the cricket. Ellery often sang for his supper. He recited poems, told tales, and was generally entertaining. His hosts were the richer for it. And Ellery got a free meal.

The Fire

IN THE SPRING OF 1844 Concord was noisy. The railroad was coming. More than a thousand Irish laborers worked sixteen-hour days, for fifty cents a day, to bring the "iron horse" into Concord. In his small red farmhouse on the outskirts of town, Ellery Channing was working on his second book of poems. "I see on the road," Ellery told Henry, "about four horse-drawn carts a day. That tells me that there are other towns nearby. Otherwise the old world lolls its tongue sleepily."

"I wish I could hear that same quiet," Henry remarked. "At our end of town, and out by Walden, the rails are ringing. One can see the railroad and the commerce it will bring. The outside world will soon be an hour from our door." He grimaced, shook his head. "Shovels, hammers, and steam-driven locomotives aren't my idea of nature."

But then neither was repetitive work. Henry was

harnessed to his own plumbago mill. In his sleep he saw lumps of graphite. Pencils danced in his dreams.

"My brain runs on pencils," he told Emerson.

"Henry, it's time for you to get away," Emerson replied. "Go off on a nice long walk somewhere."

That same fair April day, Henry went up the Sudbury River with his old friend Edward Hoar. They rowed a boat, fished, and cooked their catch on a tree stump in the woods. All went well until the wind whirled some sparks into the dry wiry grass at the foot of the stump.

Suddenly a wildfire sprang up and spread out of control. Henry and Edward raced to beat it back, but the forest floor was nothing but tinder. The flames raced well ahead of them. Their efforts to put out the fire were futile. As the wind-driven sparks popped at his feet, Henry got a board from the boat and tried to beat down the flames. The forest fire raged on up the hillside like a wild orange demon.

Edward shouted, "Where will this end?"

Henry answered, "It'll go to town."

"Then I will get there first—by boat!"

"All right. I'll go by land."

The fire grew with a wild hunger for wood. Henry ran through the smoke toward town. On the way he met a farmer and told him what had happened. The man looked sourly at Henry. "None of my stuff," he said, and stalked off.

Henry ran on for two miles. He saw Cyrus Hubbard, the owner of the woods that were burning.

"There's not much we can do against a forest fire. I'll get men and pails, and you wait here," Cyrus said. Then he ran off, while Henry stood wondering what to do. His face was blackened and sweat-streaked. As usual, Henry chose to go his own way. He trudged slowly up toward Fair Haven Cliff. Exhausted, he sat on a rock outcropping and watched the fire from on high.

Now distant bells tolled in town. Soon there were many men working madly to put out the raging fire Henry and Edward had started by mistake.

A strange, guiltless feeling came over Henry. As he saw it, the flames were consuming their natural food, wood. Fires did that. Regularly. Nature provided the wood and the lightning storm that ignited it. Henry remembered another fire from another time. He and John on their trip down the Merrimack had made camp. From distant Lowell they heard fire alarms that soft summer night. That seemed a lifetime ago—but Henry remembered it so clearly. John alive and still wooing Ellen. Henry full of promise and in love with Ellen himself.

Henry put his face in his hands and sobbed. Was he weeping over his lost brother? Or was it over the fire just below him that was eating up a three-hundred-acre wood?

Moments later, Henry dried his eyes and shook

himself out of his stupor. He wiped the soot away from his eyes with his sleeve. "I should've tended my pencils," he said bitterly. As he stood and watched, wondering which way to go, a wall of flame climbed up to meet him.

What a glorious spectacle, he thought, and am I the only one to watch it?

Now the tendrils of flame wound about the cliff. Before it, gray squirrels ran in blind haste. Wood pigeons flew heavily into the midst of the smoke. The flames brightened the pine tops. One second they flared, the next the thin limbs of the pine trees sagged like the black rigging of a pirate ship.

Henry made his decision. He hopped and jumped and zigzagged like a rabbit until he met up with the men who were beating off the forest fire. They were dousing it with water from the river. He joined them and worked until dark, when the fire finally subsided. Then he trudged home, alone. He'd never felt so defeated in his life.

That night, unable to sleep, Henry returned to the burned woods where the fire had roared. Some of the stumps still had little candles of flame sprouting from them. All around in the dull moonlight, Henry wandered amid the black waste. Finally he found the spot where he and Edward had prepared their lunch. In the murky moonlight, Henry saw the charred fish he had caught. The most costly lunch he'd never eaten.

The Hike

IN MIDSUMMER OF 1844 Henry hiked up Mount Monadnock in New Hampshire. Alone, he rambled at his own pace, eating raspberries. He had a knapsack full of books, which were as important to him as food. Sack in hand, he clumped up to a farmhouse. When the farmer's wife came to the door, Henry said, "Can you spare a little bread?"

The farmer's wife replied, "Would you take a loaf?"

"I never loaf when I'm hiking," Henry said with an impish grin. Yankee humor wasn't lost on backwoods people, who took a liking to Henry with his worn-out corduroys and biblical walking stick.

On he went, hiking, resting, reading. Sometimes, finding a clear pool, Henry took off his clothes and swam with the trout. At last he came to North Adams, in northwestern Massachusetts, and started up Mount Greylock.

The little farmhouses were fewer now, and Henry rested at one. This time a young woman came out onto the porch. She had long, shiny black hair, and she was in the midst of combing it when she saw Henry leaning on his staff by a big maple tree.

"What brings you this way?" she asked. The girl was not shy, Henry noted. She had an honest face, warm and inviting. When she began to comb her dark hair in front of him, he felt shy suddenly.

"What news do you bring of the lower world?" the girl asked with a humorous twinkle in her eye. Her dark hair sparkled in the shade of the porch as she combed it. Her eyes, Henry wondered. Where have I seen them before? Then he realized this pleasant Berkshire girl reminded him of his Ellen. As she tossed her head and plied her comb, Henry was enchanted.

"I've seen little to nothing," Henry answered. "At least little or nothing so nice as that hair of yours."

The girl stopped combing and dropped her hand to her side. Shaking her head so that her long hair swung freely, she smiled.

"Are you going up-mountain?"

Henry nodded.

"Then when you come down, you can stay with us."

"I'll be back down in a day," Henry mumbled, spellbound. But as he said it, he remembered that he was meeting Ellery Channing the next day.

"I've plans to meet someone," Henry added, by way

of excuse. Exactly what he was excusing, he did not know. She was, he decided, so much like Ellen. Right after thinking this, he changed his mind.

I do not see Ellen in her, he argued inwardly. I see only my old longing for a lost love. That being the case, I must say good-bye, here and now. And be gone.

The Berkshire girl was sorry to see him go.

"You could stay a week at our house, if you like," she called after him. However, Henry, contrary as always, passed up this chance to meet someone he might really have cared for. Compass in one hand and staff in the other, he waved good-bye to the black-haired beauty of the Greylock lowlands.

Yet long into the night, when the wind sang among the mountain laurels, Henry felt that old sadness creep back into his soul.

"Why am I most lonely when I am with others?" he asked the night wind.

But the night wind had questions of its own and didn't answer.

In the morning, as if in answer to his loneliness, the top of Mount Greylock was shrouded in a sea of fog. Henry could see nothing. And so he descended wearing an overcoat of mist and holding his compass before his nose to see where he was going. That afternoon, when the fog was gone, Henry met his friend Ellery.

At the Pittsfield railroad station they saw one another for the first time in several weeks. Momentarily,

Ellery was surprised by Henry's appearance. Unshaven and darkly tanned, Henry wore rumpled old clothes. He looked rough and ragged, and much in need of a bath.

"You look like you've already tramped to the Catskills and back," Ellery said, with a critical little wink.

Henry clapped his friend on the back. "I've eaten nothing but moonlight and fog," he said, "and I've been nowhere but up and back."

"If I didn't know you better, I'd say that you've fallen in love since I last saw you."

"I am in love," Henry vowed, "with raspberries and blueberries."

The Pond

It was Ellery Channing who, on March 5, 1845, gave Henry his push toward complete independence as a man and as a writer. Ellery wrote to Henry from New York, where he was working for the *Tribune*.

"I see nothing for you on this earth but that field, which I once named the Briars. Go out upon that, build yourself a hut, and begin the grand process of devouring yourself alive."

A grand little speech, Henry thought. He knew what Ellery meant, too. By devouring himself he would use every resource he had within him to become the writer he'd always dreamed of being.

Ellery then turned to Mr. Emerson, urging him to convince Henry to follow his muse to Walden Pond. In the end, that worked. Mr. Emerson sent Henry to the briar patch—but it was Channing who had thought it up.

What a briar patch it was, too.

Mr. Emerson's piece of Walden was eleven acres (purchased at eight dollars per acre). Later he added another three or four acres and was fond of saying that he was "Landlord and waterlord of 14 acres, more or less, on the shore of Walden, and can raise my own blackberries."

In March 1845 Thoreau began to clear the land above Walden Pond. This was his to use, Mr. Emerson said, as long as he wanted to use it. Henry would be near enough to Concord to call on friends, but he would be far enough away to feel that he was beyond the prying eyes of nosy neighbors.

"I will clear out the nettles from your briary . . . and plant pines," Thoreau told Mr. Emerson. The older man smiled beneficently. "An excellent trade. And who knows, I may very well build a lodge on the ledge across the lake. Will you help me, Henry?"

"I shall look forward to the day," Henry told his friend.

However, that day didn't come until 1847, when Henry and Bronson Alcott built a summerhouse for Mr. Emerson. As for Henry's house, his certainty was strong that he could build it very soon. So he borrowed an ax and cut down the tall, arrowy white pines from around his intended house site. These he shaped, strong and straight, for timbers, studs, and rafters. In April his house was ready to be framed, but he still had many other things to do first.

Each day Henry went to Walden with his lunch wrapped in a newspaper. He worked until sundown, and then, satisfied with his progress, walked home.

Finally he bought an old shanty, which gave him all the boards that he needed for the house. After taking it apart, he carted it—boards and nails—to Walden. Then he dug out his cellar. It was two hundred feet up from the pond on a gentle slope facing south. While digging, he ran into an abandoned woodchuck burrow. "I figure if it was good enough for him, it'll please the likes of me," Henry said to himself.

Henry dug his cellar six feet square and seven feet deep. When he reached bottom, the sand was clean and fine. "No good strong-willed potato will freeze in here," he said as the work was done. Henry was pleased with the way things were going. Not just pleased. He was thankful every step of the way. The work was good and he was fit enough to do it.

Early in May, Henry's Concord friends came out to raise the frame of his little house. Among these were Mr. Emerson, Bronson Alcott, Ellery Channing, George William Curtis and his brother Burrill, and Edmund Hosmer and his three sons. All went well, and by July Henry's solitary little house in the woods was up and ready for him to move into. However, there were still a few more things to do.

For his chimney, Henry hauled stones from Walden Pond and salvaged one thousand secondhand bricks in Concord. Building a chimney was slow, thoughtful work. The fireplace inside the cabin took Henry even more time to complete, but once the house was boarded and roofed, Henry moved right in. The date in his journal was July 4, 1845. On another line, he wrote down his expenses. These came to $28.12, and the largest part of that was for nails—$3.90.

As the summer wore on, Henry did the finishing work. He built a small woodshed to shelter firewood, and a privy, or outhouse. Finally, he carried out his own handmade furniture from his parents' house. A bed, a table, a desk, and three chairs completed the house at Walden Pond.

At last Henry was ready to settle in and write what he called his "Long Book of the Leaf": a summary of the seasons and his life at Walden. Nothing could stop him from being a writer now.

Except . . . himself.

The House

In early November, Ellery Channing came to visit at Henry's hermitage. Seeing the house for the first time, Ellery said, "Why, it's a wooden inkstand." By which he meant, of course, that Henry's house was a writer's house. Made by, and for, a writer. Ellery also noted that the house was so small that you could reach into the attic by standing on a chair and you could touch the bottom of the cellar with a broom handle. "It had no lock to the door, no curtain to the window, and belonged to nature nearly as much as to man," Ellery later wrote in his biography of Thoreau.

When Ellery came to visit, the leaves had already gone from golden to brown. "I brought you one of your mother's boiled apple puddings," Ellery said with a grin as he took a seat outside in the warm rays of the sun.

Ellery's face, a cross between a wise man's and an elf's, always had a certain cheerful look of anticipation, as if he expected nothing less than fireworks from his friends and nothing less than magic from himself.

When Henry spoke, Ellery listened. It was his habit to wait a few moments after Henry had stopped talking, just to make sure he was not about to start up again. This was both polite and practical. Ellery found what Henry had to say worth remembering.

On this particular fall day, Henry pleased Ellery with a homespun little rhyme—

> I seek the present time,
> No other chime
> Life in to-day—
> Not to sail another way,—
> To Paris or to Rome,
> Or farther still from home . . .

"Very, very nice, Henry. But what about the book you're writing?"

"Oh, it's being written. Daily. All by itself. I look and listen, and the book writes itself."

Henry made an outdoor lunch, and while the last autumn leaves lazed on their stems and the pine needles glistened, Henry roasted corn on the coals of an outdoor fire pit. He had baked bread that morning, and the two men drank fresh water from Walden Pond, and then they had the apple pudding for dessert.

"Tell me," said Ellery, after he'd finished the last

mouthful of pudding, "about this book-writing machine of yours."

"See for yourself," Henry teased in return. Then he pursed his lips. In a reedy voice, Henry said, *"Chick-a-dee-dee-dee-dee."*

At once a slate-colored bird dropped out of a pine tree and hopped onto Henry's Vermont gray coat. The small bird pecked at some threads and then did a little dance down to Henry's hand. Pinched between Henry's fingers was a soft kernel of corn. The bird took it and flew off.

"There—I have chapter one," Henry said, laughing.

"What is chapter two?" Ellery asked.

Henry stood up and went inside his house. He returned a moment later with a flute, upon which he blew a few airy notes.

Out from under Henry's house, a small brown mouse came scurrying.

Two more ethereal notes, and the mouse scampered up Henry's corduroy pants.

"Chapter two," Henry said.

Ellery, watching with fascination, started laughing.

"I guess you *are* having the book of life written for you, Henry," Ellery said. "And I congratulate you. But I bet there's more here than meets the eye. What else do you do with your time?"

"Would you have me be like our neighbors, the deer hunters, mink catchers, pigeon snatchers? All those hearty hunters and fishers who pass me by on their way to the hasty funeral of some wild animal?"

"Heavens, no," said Ellery, shaking his head. "I think I've seen what you're up to. Well, it's getting to be a little chilly."

"Why don't you spend the night with the mouse and me?"

Ellery's face lit up. His big almond eyes widened, as if it were Christmas. "Why, I'd love to! Just think—your first overnight guest. What an honor."

However, Henry's small house—ten feet wide by fifteen feet long—was too small to allow two full-grown men to sleep side by side. So Ellery, being used to woodland ways, scrunched down low and slept underneath Henry's cot.

The mouse slept in his nest beneath the house.

All the sleepers slept soundly.

The Witch

FROM THE MOMENT HE DUG into the woodchuck's burrow to build his cellar, Henry knew he was home. When he gazed deeply into the soft blue-green tints of Walden Pond, he imagined he was looking down into "the quiet parlor of the fishes."

"Ah, the pickerel of Walden," he wrote. "I am always surprised by their rare beauty, as if they were fabulous fishes. . . . They possess a quite dazzling and transcendent beauty . . . the pearls, the animal nuclei or crystals of the Walden water. They, of course, are Walden all over and all through."

Ellery Channing wasn't the only one who visited Henry. Often there were children from the village who liked the same things Henry did—the birds, the fishes, and the animals. Frederick Willis, George Keyes, and Tom Hosmer, all former students of Henry's, came out pretty often, and they brought fresh pies from his mother's kitchen.

Normally Henry told them stories and took them out in his little boat. There, floating on the clear water, Henry played his flute as the pickerel moved under them and his notes echoed through the hills above.

The still boat was also a perfect place to tell the children the story of the squaw who once lived there at Walden. "She escaped from her village one night and came upon some evil men talking of war. She made the earth rumble a warning to them, and down came the stones from the hillside, forming the shoreline of Walden Pond."

"Is that how it came to be Walden?" asked George.

"Well," said Henry, blowing a little note on his flute, "some say it's called 'Walled-In' because of that."

"Do you believe it?" asked Tom.

"I believe everything. I'm so susceptible to belief that I have no original ideas of my own."

Tom wondered what all that meant. "Mr. Emerson told my father that you're the most original thinker in Concord."

"The most original tootler?"

"Could you tell us another story?" George begged.

Henry blew a soft breath into his flute. A jay screamed in the woods. Henry chuckled, put the flute on his lap. "Well, once there was a demon that lived here by the lake. He came to the local farms to ask for work. Then he robbed and murdered the farmers and came back here to hide."

The three children looked over their shoulders.

"What was the demon's name?" Tom demanded.

Henry snorted. "He was called Mr. Rum. I found one of his kind—an earthen jug—buried where I planted my beans the other day." Henry went on. "He lived in a jug, Mr. Rum did. And he still lives in bottles in town today. Look out for him, Tom, for he travels far and lays you low at the first opportunity." Henry rowed the children across the pond and came ashore.

Later on, Henry and his guests ate Cynthia Thoreau's peach pie. Between mouthfuls, Tom asked Henry if he ever got lonely.

"Why do you ask that Tom?"

"Well, you've got nobody to live with but yourself."

Henry said, "Is that so?" Finishing his pie, he stood up and whistled a low, curious note.

Immediately, a woodchuck came running from a nearby burrow.

The children squealed with pleasure as the woodchuck waddled among them. After he was fed some pie, he went off, and Henry whistled again, long and low. This time a gray squirrel scampered down a tree, and yet another whistle summoned a glossy black crow that dropped out of a tree and sat on Henry's shoulder.

"How could I ever be lonely in a place like this?" Henry asked Tom, who shrugged and said, "Don't ask me."

"Yeah," the others put in, "Henry's got loads of friends—even more than you, Tom."

The crow cawed. Henry fed him a piece of crust, and the gray squirrel, too. The whistle he used to send them away was different from his summons call. Henry told his animal friends when the visit was over, and they departed as they came.

"I would show you my mouse," Henry offered, "but it's past his bedtime."

The Jail

OF ALL THE THINGS Henry planned to do while living at Walden, spending a night in jail was not one of them. Nevertheless, one summer evening, that is where he found himself.

"You've forgotten to pay your poll tax again," Sam Staples reminded him when they met on Main Street in Concord. Sam, the town tax collector and jailer, was a friend of Henry's, but his patience was wearing thin.

"I'm going to the cobbler's to have my shoe repaired—so my money's all spent this night. Sorry, Sam." Henry's tone wasn't the least bit apologetic.

Sam shook his head and shrugged. "I'll pay your tax, Henry, if you're that hard up."

"I'd be hard up only if I *had* to pay. But I don't. The tax is wrong, Sam. You and the selectmen know that perfectly well. A tax that is used to enforce slavery and promote war in Mexico is not one I'm going to contribute to."

"Never?" Sam's eyebrows went up.

"Well, *never* is a strong, long word, Sam. But, no, I don't think I ever will pay for a war that I don't believe in—or any war, for that matter."

Sam's troubled face turned sour. "Henry, if you don't pay, I shall have to lock you up pretty soon."

"Well, now's as good as any other time, Sam. I'm not going to pay."

"You're deviling me, young man." Sam's face hardened some more.

"I would sooner man a devil than devil a man. But anyway, you're welcome to have me." Henry put out his hands.

"Then come along, Henry."

Henry followed Sam to the three-story granite building with its surrounding ten-foot brick wall mounted with sharp iron pickets. Once Henry was inside his cell, his cell mate spoke up.

"What're you in for?" he asked.

"Resisting, though I did not resist the charge. I went willingly."

The man's face screwed tight. "That makes no more sense than what I'm in here for."

"What's that, sir?"

"I'm *accused* of burning down a barn."

"*Did* you?"

"I burned it down, but not on purpose."

Henry said, "I resisted our bloody war in Mexico, a war that is paid for by taxes—*my* taxes."

Henry's cell mate spat on the stone floor of the jail. "Been three months in here, all told." The man smiled. "I don't mind it at all."

"Why's that?"

The jailed man gave Henry a gap-tooth grin. "Free room and board, though I go out and work the hay fields during the day, just like usual. That Sam is a mighty fine man."

"Yes, he most certainly is," Henry confirmed. "He could've tossed me in here three months ago, if he'd a mind to."

After a while Henry stretched out on his cot and slept. Late in the night, however, he wakened to a pitiful voice crying mournfully into the darkness, "What is life?" The voice came from another cell.

No other prisoner saw fit to answer.

Silence.

Then again—"What is life?"

This time, though, the man sought to answer his own question—"So . . . *this* . . . is life!"

For some reason, or unreason, Henry got up, pressed his face to the bars of the cell and asked, loud and clear, "Well, then, what is life?"

Somewhere a dog barked. Then a cock crowed. A snore started up in one of the neighboring cells.

"The stars are fainter in town," Henry whispered to himself.

There was no further response to life's most puzzling question, so Henry went back to his cot.

"I know what life is," Henry said aloud. "Life is a good night's sleep." He chuckled to himself.

Then he closed his eyes and slept without waking.

In the morning the prisoners were given hot chocolate and bread. Henry accepted his eagerly. His cell mate gobbled down his bread and quaffed his chocolate, spilling some of it on his beard as he swallowed noisily. Wiping his lips with his sleeve, the man said to Henry, "I don't think I'll be seeing you tonight."

"Oh? Why is that?"

"Sam said your fine's been paid."

Henry gazed openly at his cell mate, wondering if it could be true.

"You never said if you committed your crime," Henry stated.

The man hitched his shoulders and shook his head. "Said I *did*, and *didn't*—an' that's the truth. You see, I was smokin', and the little bit of ash caught some straw and started a fire. I'm as innocent of burning—by intent—as you are of not paying your taxes."

Henry swirled the last of his chocolate around in his tin cup, and then he swallowed it down.

"No, I am guilty as charged."

"We all got to pay our taxes," the man agreed.

"No. Not if we don't think they're right."

His cell mate shuffled toward the iron door and clanged it once with his tin cup. While he waited, he said some parting words to Henry. "What if we all thought that way? Up and withheld our taxes. Why just think of the hell it would cause!"

"Think of the heaven it would bring, with no slavery and no war. No bloodshed, no murder. Just a dead tax."

A voice came from outside the cell. "Are you talking to Henry Thoreau?" Sam Staples unlocked the iron door with a jangle of keys. "You watch—he's going to be mad as the devil when I tell him he's free to go."

The cell mate laughed, and left to work in the hay fields.

"Did Mr. Emerson pay my taxes? Is that it, Sam?" Henry looked accusingly at Sam, as if he'd arranged it himself.

"Tell you the truth, Henry, I couldn't see who it was—too dark last night to tell. My daughter took the money, anyways. Someone said it was your Aunt Maria paid it up."

"Last night?" Henry guffawed. "You slept with my bail money under your pillow while I was here in this buggy building?"

"Not really. But I had my boots off, and I figured, why wake a sleeping resister. He's just going to resist some more." Sam winked at Henry.

"I would like to know who put up the money, Sam. I really would."

"Well, I can't say if it was a he or a she. Can't say if they was short or tall, big or small, well dressed or plain, shawled or coated, young or old—couldn't rightly say. Nor could anyone else, cause no one else was there except that one or two or possibly three small or large donors at the door. And like I said, my daughter met them, not me. So there you have it, Henry, like it or leave it. Anyways, you can't stay here another minute."

There was nothing more to say about it, so Henry gave up and went out onto the morning streets of Concord, and took care of his shoe. A half hour later he was back at Walden picking huckleberries on a hill. "The state is nowhere to be seen," he bellowed.

A couple of crows announced their pleasure at Henry's release. Back in Concord, word went around the town that Henry Thoreau, that patriotic New England native son, didn't believe in slavery, the war in Mexico, or the United States government poll tax that supported them.

When Mr. Emerson saw Henry a few days after his lockup, he asked him, "Why did you go to jail?"

Henry simply replied, "Why did you not?"

The Words

HENRY LIVED CONTENTEDLY with his animal family at Walden Pond. For money, he built fireplaces and fences, painted houses, and did carpentry. He also sowed, hoed, and harvested, both for himself and for others. However, his main work, in his own words, was "self-appointed inspector of snow-storms and rain-storms . . . surveyor if not of highways, then of forest paths and acres."

In reality, Henry was a skilled surveyor. Most of his spending money came from surveying his neighbors' farms. He loved being out in the open air, and the logic of finding lost property lines appealed to him. This also led him to fields where he found new flowers and old Indian relics.

Much of the time that he was at Walden, Henry spent walking around. In the chestnut groves he found nuts. In the pond he found fish, though he stopped catching them because he thought they were so lovely where they were. He loved "playing the flute, and watching the perch, which I seem to have charmed, hovering around me, and the moon traveling over the ribbed bottom, which was strewn with the wrecks of the forest."

Hearing the exultant note of a bird, the earliest buzz of a bee, the faintest chirp of a frog—hearing these, according to Henry, was also his work. Yet for all of these, his payment was love, not cash.

Henry did earn some real money by lecturing. But as far as he was concerned, he wasn't very good at it. "I fail to get even the attention of the average person. I should suit them better if I suited myself less."

The public wanted average thoughts instead of original ones. "I would rather that my audience came to me than that I should go to them."

As it happened, Henry's audience did come to him, and to Walden. But they got their talks for free.

He had only three chairs, but they were often in use. When these weren't enough, Henry and his guests retired to his parlor in the pines. In warmer weather his parlor was full of wayfaring visitors.

When Ellery came by and found that Henry wasn't at home, he always left him a leaf, which he slid under his door to tell him he'd been calling.

Henry roamed about the woods, meadows, and hills. Often he met his neighbors on their farms and in front of their huts—woodcutters, masons, stonecutters, and bridge workers. Henry wrote down his conversations with them in his journal. There was the old revolutionary soldier who said he loved the good healthy smell of gunpowder. There was the drunk who slept in the rain because it didn't matter to him if he was wet or dry. There was the neighbor whose hill farm was such poor stuff that it was set up just "to hold the world together." It was not useful; it was just there.

Sometimes Henry's journeys in the field took him to obscure hollows where a certain shy flower could be seen only at a certain time of year. Once, bringing a pine tree (roots and all) to his mother, Henry toted the big tree on his shoulder and walked past the church. He'd completely forgotten it was Sunday. As he strode by, all the parishioners were staring after him as if he were some kind of monster. "I forgot it was Sunday," he told Cynthia later on. "And to think, fifty years ago I'd have been locked in a pillory for ignoring God's day of rest."

In winter, because no visitors came to see Henry at Walden, he had the world all to himself. And it was then he could say, perhaps only to his mouse, "My work is writing."

Free from distraction, safe and warm in his tight little inkstand of a house, Henry used his writing time wisely. At the end of his two-year stay at Walden, in 1847, he had completed the better part of two books, *A Week on the Concord and Merrimack Rivers* and *Walden; or, Life in the Woods.*

A Week was a record of the memorable boat trip

he'd taken with his brother John. *Walden* was the story of his life in the midst of nature.

Henry recorded everything that happened to him, from scrubbing the floor to scribbling verses. He wrote about how far a honeybee would fly to get a meal of goldenrod and aster blossom. Henry trapped a bee and dusted its fuzz with red powder. Then, setting it free, he watched the bee rise and wend its way toward town. In less than half an hour, that same red-furred bee was back at Walden Pond.

"He may have gone more than three quarters of a mile. At any rate, he had a head wind to contend with while laden. They fly swiftly and surely to their nest, never resting by the way, and I was surprised—though I had been informed of it—at the distance to which the village bees go for flowers."

So the years of work at Walden—of trying to see what life was really like and how he might write about it—bore their fruit. He had written his book of seasons. After two years in the woods, he felt full. It was Ellery Channing who had said, "Devour yourself alive!" Henry had been like a starved man when he came there, but now he had eaten his fill.

Now, in September 1847, he felt a stirring inside him. An urge to create a new life. He itched to get out upon the road with no fixed house where people would ask, "Is Henry at home?"

In *Walden* he wrote, "I left the woods for as good a

reason as I went there. Perhaps, it seemed to me that I had several lives to live, and could not spare more time for that one."

Those who knew Henry saw the difference in him. He was a changed man. As Mr. Emerson said, "He was a student when he went to Walden; when he returned to Concord, he was a teacher."

Teacher or not, Henry wanted to be a writer.

Yet it was only after six attempts to get *A Week* and *Walden* accepted by a publisher that Henry finally got a contract for both books, from Wiley & Putnam, Publishers. However, the printing costs for *A Week* were to come out of Henry's own pocket. *Walden*, they said, would come out at a later date.

Henry felt despondent. How could he afford to finance the publication of his own book? He felt like a failure. His friend Mr. Emerson was paid for his books. Why wasn't Henry?

His Aunt Maria echoed Henry's fears and doubts. "*Walden* isn't really publishable," she said. "There are parts in there that sound like blasphemy."

Henry knew what she meant. His church in the woods, without a deacon or a hymnal, wasn't her way—it was his. It seemed wrong to her for Henry to tell the world that anyone, or everyone, should experience such lonely exultation.

Henry's mother joined in. *Walden* was not her cup of tea either. Then Aunt Maria cast the book out entirely by saying, "I don't think *Walden* will ever sell enough copies to pay back your publisher. You'll be out the money—or someone else will."

Henry's voice trembled with anger as he replied, "When have I not paid my way?"

It hurt him to think his writing meant so little to his family. But that was the way it was. They didn't think much of him as a writer.

In the end, as Aunt Maria had predicted, Henry went into debt. Of the 1,000 copies of *A Week* that were printed, 706 went into the Thoreaus' attic. Undiscouraged, Henry worked on *Walden*, still hoping to prove his aunt wrong. He revised it seven times. Ticknor & Fields accepted the book for publication. But although *Walden* was praised by reviewers, it sold very modestly. Henry's two years, two months, and two days at Walden Pond gave birth to a book that sold fewer than 2,000 copies.

"Maybe I wasn't meant to be a writer," Henry decided. "Maybe it's good enough that I am just a man."

But he had to keep telling himself that, because he still wanted to be a writer.

The Calling

MANY TOWNSPEOPLE wanted to know why Henry had gone to jail. This got him more attention than his two published books. In fact, he was asked so often about this that he wrote and delivered a lecture on the subject. It was called "The Relation of the Individual to the State," and he delivered it at the Concord Lyceum in the month of January 1848.

The audience liked the talk so much that Henry delivered a second one three weeks later. More townspeople came to the second lecture, and all agreed that Henry had something to say.

A year later, Henry published his two talks in a single essay called "Resistance to Civil Government." His one night in jail had turned into an odd but effective calling card.

"What's that I hear?" asked a schoolmaster when

Henry came to the post office. "Are you opposed to government?"

Henry said, "No, but I would rather go to jail than submit to an unfair law that takes away the freedoms granted to us by the Constitution."

The schoolmaster didn't like the sound of that. But he didn't know why. "Is that it?" he asked.

"There's more," Henry continued. "Every American citizen ought to consult his conscience about the taxes given to support the wrongful war in Mexico. Taxation leads to more human enslavement. As for me, I'll have none of it."

"That's anarchy," said the schoolmaster, who reminded Henry of the old-fashioned whipping master at Concord Academy.

Naturally, there was antislavery talk at Henry's parents' house—Cynthia and her sister Louisa. Aunt Jane and Aunt Maria were members of the Concord Women's Anti-Slavery Society, and they were very vocal. But only Henry went to jail for his beliefs. On this he stood alone, and though some hated him for it, others admired him just as much.

In October 1851 Henry and his family brought an escaped slave named Henry Williams into their house and hid him there. Henry stayed up all night while Williams slept. From time to time, Henry stood up from the chair by his bedside and looked out the window to make sure that no one was coming. In the morning,

Williams woke with a start. He jumped up and was ready to run in the bedclothes Henry had given him.

"Are they coming?" he asked, wild-eyed.

"No," Henry said. "No one is coming."

"Am I safe?"

"You slept through the night. The only caller was a barred owl who hooted five times."

Williams sat back down on the bed and rubbed his head. "There's a writ out for my arrest," he said softly.

"How did you get here?"

"I came on foot."

"Your feet must be sore." Henry sat beside Henry Williams on the bed. "Why don't you let me bathe them for you?" he asked.

At this, the other man lifted his brows in amazement. "You would do that for *me*—a slave, a wanted man?" Henry Williams sighed. "You must be the *kindest*—and all-out *craziest*—man I ever met. Go ahead, wash my feet, if you want to. Lord knows, they've been down some hard, dusty roads. And they need washing."

When his feet were washed, Henry Williams accepted a new suit of clothes and then had a huge breakfast of pancakes, eggs, and ham.

Before noon Henry walked with Henry Williams to the train station, where he saw a depot agent in plain clothes. Henry Williams's skin was light in color, and his clothes spoke only of good fortune, but nonetheless he was given a stare because he was a stranger, and a dark one at that. Henry put things at ease, however, by speaking and gesturing in a way that suggested a very old friendship with Henry Williams.

"That was a close call," Henry Williams whispered when the depot agent walked away.

"There was a Boston policeman under that calm gaze and corduroy coat," Henry observed, "but we fooled him all right."

"Sometimes," Henry Williams said, "I just want to run when I see a man like that. Just run and follow the North Star the way I always do."

Henry smiled. "We'll let the railroad train take you to the North Star," he said. "And speaking of the train, here it comes now."

They shook hands, and Henry Williams got ready to leave.

"Wait," Henry said, "you almost forgot your hat."

As he handed it to him, Henry noticed a bit of moss inside the crown. "Do you collect woods stuff, too?"

"No, sir. That little bit of fluff that you see there is some turf from the mother of all creation, the ground on which we walk. We believe that if we want to get to Canada in one piece, we got to have that little bit of earth with us. Our success depends on it."

Henry grinned. "I feel that way myself, and I shall be carrying some in my hat for you from now on."

"Bless you, sir." Henry Williams touched Henry Thoreau's shoulder. "I'll never forget you," he said as he stepped onto the train going north.

This wasn't the first or the last time that Henry or his parents aided an escaped slave. For some years Henry's life was devoted to caring for runaways. He always sat beside them while they slept at night, in case they should be discovered. When he met John Brown, the great freedom fighter and abolitionist, Henry was awed. Here, at last, was a man who fought for what he believed in. Henry was moving toward the belief that force might be necessary to end the institution of slavery.

The Revolutionary

HENRY MET JOHN BROWN in the winter of 1857. His friend Frank Sanborn brought Brown straight to Henry's door for dinner. Brown was traveling through Massachusetts raising money for his cause. As an abolitionist who hated slavery, Brown was both loved and reviled.

And for good reason. He did not merely protest against slavery; he and his sons fought violently against it. They bore arms and freed slaves on the plantations in Missouri. It was well known he'd murdered many a slave master in close-quarters fighting. "The work of the Lord," Brown called it that steely cold day when he and Henry first laid eyes on each other.

Henry was not prepared for this fiery-eyed prophet who sat in a straight-backed chair before the Thoreaus' fireplace.

"I had twenty sons," Brown told Henry. "Eight

died in childhood. The others are men just like me, fighters. Not one of them would hesitate to lay his life down to free a slave." Brown paused and looked around the room. "God teaches us that one man should not own another man," he said in his gravelly voice.

Someone said "Amen," and Henry nodded.

Brown looked large for the chair. His legs were thrust out before him. He wore a suit of clothes that seemed too small for him. His furrowed face was lean and brown from the sun. Henry noticed that his starched cuffs came short of his thick-boned wrists. Brown's hair glowed white as wool and was piled on his head in snowy drifts. His beard, too, was white, and it hung below his chest. Altogether he was an amazing man to see and to hear, and Henry was completely absorbed by him.

However, it wasn't Brown's face or clothes that mesmerized Henry. It was the man's eyes. They shone with such a passion Henry thought they looked like two blue sapphires. It also seemed to him, as he listened to Brown speak, that this deliverer of slaves was not long for this life. That he was soon to die.

Brown did not seem to care. "Somewhere in the mountains of West Virginia," he said in a voice like a wild wind, "I will have my base of operations, a place where slaves all over the South can join our army."

"What will you do with your army, sir?" Henry asked.

"Do?" Brown barked. He blinked in disbelief. "Why, I'll prepare them for an invasion of the South."

"Is that practical?" Frank Sanborn queried. "I mean, can it really be done?"

Brown's blue eyes hawked about the room, ravaging each listener.

Each man, Henry thought, who feels those hot eyes on him knows what it is like to be struck by lightning. Henry did. He felt it in his very soul. Brown had him.

"Once my operation is started," Brown continued, "all slaves throughout the South will rise up against their masters and join us in a triumphant march to freedom. Jubilant Negroes will join us at every mile, and our stream of men will swell until it is a mighty river indeed. And when it is so, it will roar like Niagara."

A small polite flutter of applause followed this poetic retort. Brown paid no attention to it. His eyes momentarily fastened on Henry's. "And you, sir, what would you do at this historic hour?" Brown wanted to know.

Henry's face colored deep red.

"I would not keep everyone waiting," he said, and Brown, for the first time, smiled warmly at him, as if recognizing a long-lost friend.

John Brown's Bowie Knife

WHEN JOHN BROWN was captured at Harper's Ferry two years later, Henry announced that he would speak in Brown's behalf at the church in Concord. "Someone must speak out in Brown's defense," he told his mother, "and I fear no one will unless I do."

"Yes, Henry, you undoubtedly shall. But you know the Republican Town Committee is against your talk."

Henry laughed. "Who else fears freedom of speech?"

Cynthia Thoreau poured Henry a cup of tea. "The local abolitionists think you'll go too far. They think you will lose the ones who might choose to take your side. Many think Brown is too revolutionary."

Henry rattled his cup in his saucer. "How far is too far when freedom is at stake?"

Seeing her son's face so flushed and angry, Cynthia said, to calm him down, "We abolitionists must be careful not to set them against us, Henry. The town committee is strong. They could go against us when we need to lean on them for support, if it comes to that."

"I'd rather not lean on a falling tree," Henry told her.

Later that day, a selectman with a pinched face told Henry, "I don't think conditions are favorable for your lecture."

"Oh? Why?" Henry pretended he had no idea.

"Well," said the flustered selectman, "Brown is going to be hanged, no matter what you say or do. Even the liberal papers are calling him 'misguided, wild, and apparently insane.'"

"Liberal papers, you say? That's just another majority opinion. We must think for ourselves, sir."

"Well, what are you going to do then?" the man asked nervously.

"I'll go ahead with my talk as planned."

The selectman didn't know how to respond, but he managed to mutter, "I don't think you quite understand. We don't want you to speak publicly."

Henry shrugged and said, "But I didn't ask you for your opinion. I'm asking you to announce that I'm going to speak."

Hearing this, the man stared at Henry as if he were a madman. Then he turned and walked stiffly up the road.

Henry knew that even narrow-minded selectmen couldn't, by law, refuse his right to free speech in Town Hall. But they could refuse to ring the summons bell that called the town to Henry's meeting.

Henry took that in his stride, too. He rang the bell himself.

That night he delivered the speech of his life. Calling it "A Plea for Captain John Brown," Henry brought tears to the eyes of the liberals and snorts out of the mouths of some conservatives. From where he stood at the podium, he noticed nothing, however. His voice carried the words and visions of the prophet-eyed man whom he'd admired from the day he met him. John Brown was with him that night.

Edward Emerson, Mr. Emerson's teenage son, was in attendance that night. Born three years after Waldo died, Edward had as much fondness and admiration for Henry as did his father. After the hall had emptied out and all the people had left, Henry asked him, "Did you like it?"

Edward said admiringly, "I felt the paper in your hands was going to burst into flame."

"It burned my fingers . . . but what did the others think, I wonder, the ones who need to hear the message most?"

Edward gave Henry a small hug. "You mean you don't know? Many of those who came to scoff stayed to pray. You moved practically everyone, Henry."

Henry threw his arm around the boy, who had once

asked him to be his father. "Well, then, we've done the best we could."

One month later, when it became clear that Brown was going to be hanged, Henry asked permission to ring the bell at the precise hour of his death. He was refused. Still the service went forward as planned. But no sooner was it over than news came that a fugitive from Brown's band had turned up in Boston. He was mistakenly put on a train, which went to Concord.

Thoreau was enlisted to take this fugitive, a white man named Francis Jackson Merriam, by horse and buggy to board a train going to Canada. He picked up Merriam in a buggy borrowed from Mr. Emerson.

On the way to the station, Merriam exclaimed, "We have to return to Concord at once!" His face looked crazed, Henry thought.

"What for?" Henry's voice was steady and calm.

"I need to ask Mr. Emerson for something."

Henry urged the horse on. "Giddup."

Merriam protested again. "I need something."

"What is it you need? Maybe I can help."

Merriam's eyes gleamed. "Mr. Emerson will back us," he said. "We got to return to Harper's Ferry. It's the only way."

"What will you do there?"

"Fight 'em again. This time we'll win."

Henry pursed his lips, said nothing. The horse trotted on in the darkness. The dim light of a passing farmhouse glowed across a fog-bound field.

"Why don't you stop, Mr. Emerson?"

Henry glanced at the rawboned, crazy-voiced man sitting beside him in the buggy. Again Henry said nothing. The horse's hooves dislodged a stone in the road. One wheel rolled heavily over it, and the buggy lurched. Merriam bumped against Henry, his head almost hitting Henry's chin. The two men looked carefully at one another.

"Are you Emerson?" Merriam asked.

"I'm not."

Merriam came even closer to Henry and studied his face. "Are you positive?"

"I wouldn't lie to you." Henry maintained his close eye contact.

Suddenly the man started to weep. "No, of course, you wouldn't do that." Then, after a long silence, in which the horse shook his tack and nickered softly, Merriam asked quietly, "Who are you then?"

"I am Henry Thoreau, standing in for Mr. Emerson."

Merriam, his lower jaw thrust out, seemed about to challenge Henry, but then the fight went out of him and he slumped forward, elbows on knees.

Henry clicked his tongue against the roof of his mouth, and the horse trotted on into the night, heading for the South Acton train station. Once there, Henry scouted the station and, finding it empty, got Merriam a ticket and put him on the train to Canada.

On the way home along the foggy road, Henry

spoke to himself. Or perhaps to the horse, whose ears flicked rhythmically to the soft syllables of his speech. Henry said, "By aiding a fugitive, I've become one. It's strange. Today I listened to the howling of a wild dog, yet I didn't become that dog. Why am I to be so loved and yet so unloved by my fellow man for merely wanting all men to be free?"

The night wind moaned. The horse shook at the reins. The fog closed all around Henry and reminded him of the lonely night he'd spent on Mount Greylock. He buggied on through the darkness.

Some months after John Brown was hanged at the gallows at Charlestown, Virginia, Henry read of his hero's last words. Brown had been taken in a farm wagon drawn by two white horses to the place of his death. In the back of the wagon was a plain pine coffin. Brown sat on it, his hands and legs shackled.

After the guards freed him to walk to the gallows, Brown looked around and said, "I'm glad it's a beautiful day. Please do not make me wait too long."

At a signal from the commanding officer, Brown was hanged. A few days later his sons and companions were put to death in the same way.

Reading this in a letter from Frank Sanborn, Henry burst into tears. He had not cried this way since the death of his brother John. Sometime after this, Brown's family sent Henry a special gift. When he opened the box, he found inside it John Brown's bowie knife.

The Indian

STRANGERS, MEETING HENRY for the first time, saw a man of average build with unusually large arms. He had a windburned complexion, and he wore clay-colored corduroys that blended in with the woods. Henry said he saw more minks that way. According to some observers, Henry was more animal than man. But he often lay in bed for weeks at a time. The bouts of tuberculosis, which afflicted all of the Thoreaus, were part of Henry's inheritance.

In July 1857 Henry went to Maine with his old friend and woods burner, Edward Hoar. In Bangor they met a Penobscot Indian guide, Joe Polis, who took them on a river trip that Henry remembered with special affection for the rest of his life.

"How much would you charge for taking us out in your canoe?" Henry asked Joe.

"Two dollars a day," Joe answered.

Henry bargained for a better price. "I myself get only a dollar a day for surveying," he said.

Joe asked, "Is that my fault?" Then he tapped his pipe on his palm, refilled it, and asked Henry for a light.

Henry struck a match and lit Joe's pipe.

After drawing deeply and spreading smoke in the various directions, Joe said, "I have reconsidered, Mr. Thoreau. I'll take you out for a dollar fifty a day, and at the end of the week, you give me fifty cents more for my canoe."

That seemed like a deal to Henry, and Edward nodded his approval.

At four the next morning, they launched their canoe near Deer Island on Moosehead Lake. Their breakfast was hard-bread, fried pork, and strong coffee.

"Can you teach me your Indian words for such things as paddle, canoe, mountain, and river?" Henry asked Joe.

Joe nodded. "If you like, I can do that."

"I would like that very much," Henry said.

Joe smiled with his eyes and nodded again, and then the three men spent the rest of that day paddling on Moosehead Lake. By noon they reached Mount Kineo. There, Joe, Edward, and Henry made camp. Joe went off with a hand line and a hook and came back shortly with a beautiful trout.

They passed a pleasant afternoon and evening in that camp, listening to loons crying in the night. Henry woke up once when it was still dark and saw a strange glowing on the forest floor. He had never seen such a thing. The logs and ferns and stones burned with a ghostly pallor. For the longest time, Henry crawled about on all fours, looking at the lovely phosphorescence. He sniffed it like a dog, rubbed it on his hands, and the thing still gave off a sparkle.

What is it?

Henry didn't know. In all of his woodland experience, he had never seen anything like it before.

Silently, he slipped back under his blankets. Outside, the ferns glimmered, teasing Henry with the question, what is this?

Looking through the tent flap at the trembling stars, Henry asked himself—"What is brighter, the ground or the sky? Heaven is below as well as above."

Joe seemed to be asleep, but he had seen Henry poking around in the dark. "What you see out there?" he wanted to know.

"The ground's all lit up," Henry said.

"Fox fire," said Joe, softly laughing. "It lives on old wet wood. Now, go to sleep."

The next morning they finished the voyage across the lake, and after portaging the canoe through a fir forest, the men launched it again in the Penobscot River. A day of rest followed, and they set off again. This time they went on the Umbazooksus River. Henry sat in front of Joe, with Edward at the bow. Joe, while paddling hard, accidentally spat on Henry's back.

"I felt that," Henry said. "And it wasn't rain."

Joe laughed. "Sorry," he said. Then, after a little

while, Joe told Henry that when a man spits by mistake on someone's back, it means that person is going to get married.

Henry paddled on in silence. "I don't think I'm going to get married, Joe," he said after some time.

"You're not? Why?"

"I had my chance."

Joe said, "There are other chances."

But Henry shook his head. "In my case, there was only one," he said knowingly.

Later that same day, Edward and Henry got separated from Joe, who went on ahead of them, carrying the canoe by himself. Stumbling through foot-deep water and mud, Edward told Henry, "I can't believe we are paying for this trip."

"We're gaining knowledge," Henry answered, as he swatted a mosquito on his cheek.

"Yes," Edward agreed. "You've learned you're going to get married, and I've learned that I don't like camping as much as I thought I did."

They both laughed.

A while later they weren't laughing anymore. Both men were totally lost. "I can't see Joe's tracks anymore," Henry said, with his nose bent to the ground.

"It's almost dark," Edward said, "and we never had our noon meal."

"—unless you count the mosquitoes we've been eating."

Henry and Edward laughed.

Then Edward called, "Halloo—" Both men listened to his echo bounce away into the hills.

A snorting noise, a woofing bearlike cough, came back on the tail end of Henry's echo. And then, out from behind a nearby tree, Joe showed his face.

"I thought you two were woodsmen," he said, smiling.

"We used to be," Henry answered.

"Camp's up ahead," Joe told him, "and I have some food cooking. By the way, how did you get so muddy?"

Henry looked at Edward. He was brown from his head to his feet. Then he took stock of himself. He too was a muddy mess. All three had a good chuckle over this, and then they hiked on in the twilight until they came to Joe's cozy little camp on Chamberlain Lake.

At the end of their camping trip in the Maine wilderness, they had covered 325 miles. Henry had learned how to make a birch-bark candle, how to make checkerberry and hemlock tea, and how to eat mosquitoes. He had measured the carcass of a moose that Joe Polis shot and skinned. On the last night they were together, Joe leaned over to Henry and whispered something to him. Henry nodded and smiled.

"What was that he said to you?" Edward later asked, when they were on the night boat heading back to Boston.

Henry smiled. "I'll never tell."

"Not even your oldest friend?"

Henry looked fondly at Edward. "Joe gave me an Indian name, that's all."

Edward said, "Oh? And what is it?"

"You're not supposed to spread it around, the name. But I'll tell you this—in English it means "great paddler.""

Edward said, "And to think all this time I've been calling you Great Muddler."

The Country

ON FEBRUARY 3, 1859, Henry's father, John Thoreau, died after a two-year illness. Henry took over the failing pencil business and managed to sell the family-owned graphite mill. For this he got more than his father was getting for the pencils. Henry also continued as a surveyor and lecturer, and wrote in his endless journal, which now filled many notebooks.

By August 1861, at age forty-four, Henry appeared much older than he was. A great sadness filled him, and this sorrow was noticeable to all who knew him. "I have been sick so long," he told a friend, "that I have forgotten how it feels to be well." Yet he also noted, "It occurs to me that probably in different states of what we call health, even in morbid states, we are peculiarly fitted for certain investigations." This was, perhaps, particularly true of Thoreau. When feeling ill, he could think deeply and clearly. And his sensitivity, when sick, was acute. His thoughts about conservation were something of an obsession with him now. Soil erosion, and the loss of trees to lumber and building and the railroad, concerned him. The English fur-trade industry and the American muskrat hunting were cruel and wasteful, Henry thought. Why couldn't people understand the fragility of nature?

He wrote—"There is no other land; there is no other life but this." And he went off into the woods and measured the life of an ancient cedar stump by its rings. The idea that a tree could live for hundreds of years was unusual in his time. By looking at the annual rings of stumps, Henry was able to see the history of the Concord forest. It was Henry's unique idea, too, to find a way to preserve such forests to create public parks for the future. He wrote, "Each town should have a park, or rather a primitive forest, of five hundred or a thousand acres, where a stick should never be cut for fuel. . . . Let us keep the New World *new*, preserve all the advantages of living in the country."

Henry's last journal entry was in 1861. He wrote about the pockmarks left in the dirt after a rainstorm. By examining each indentation closely, Henry found the direction from which the rain had come: "distinct to an observant eye, and yet . . . unnoticed by most."

Closing his journal, he closed, as well, a lifelong habit of writing down what he saw around him. His whispery voice in the coming months of weakness would be his final way of communicating what he knew, what he felt, and the strength of his faith.

"Red-tailed hawks," he told a friend, "are common in Concord, yet unknown at the seashore twenty miles away."

Asked about the future, Henry blinked. "Just as uninteresting as ever," he joked. Then he added, "You've been skating on this river; perhaps I'm going to skate on some other." After a little while, Henry smiled and said, "Perhaps I'm going up country."

It was at the end of March 1862 that Henry's old jailer, Sam Staples, dropped in for a visit. He found Henry radiant and sitting upright in his bed, which had been moved downstairs to the living room so Henry could be more in the midst of people.

After his visit Sam told Mr. Emerson, "I never saw a man dying with so much pleasure and peace."

Mr. Emerson, remembering his own recent meeting with Henry, said, "He spoke to me of chickadees and the ice at Walden, which will soon be melting, and the coming of the spring birds."

Sam shook his head and sighed. "Few men in Concord know Mr. Thoreau."

"Do you know him, Sam?"

"More than most, less than some. But I'll tell you this, I came away today feeling better than when I entered his door."

"Why is that?" Mr. Emerson asked, even though he knew the answer. He wanted to hear it from Sam's lips.

"Henry made me feel more alive, and that's not something many dying men can do."

"Maybe our Henry isn't dying," Mr. Emerson suggested, after a moment's silence. "Maybe he's just going 'up county,' as he says himself."

The End

ON MAY 6, 1862, Edward Hoar's father brought Henry a bouquet of hyacinths from his garden. Henry smelled them and said he liked them very much. A little while later he closed his eyes. His mother, sister Sophia, and Aunt Louisa watched as Henry's breathing grew fainter. Finally his lips parted. Gently he said, "Moose." Then, after this word, he said another, "Indian."

Then Henry Thoreau was gone.

Aunt Sophia broke the silence by saying, "I feel as if something very beautiful has happened—not death."

The other family members agreed. In spite of what had happened, in spite of Henry's passing, the room seemed full of life.

When Ellery Channing heard the news, he was greatly saddened but not surprised, because he had been at Henry's side so many times in the past few months.

"Half the world died for me . . . . None of it looks the same as when I looked at it with him."

At Henry's funeral on May 9, Mr. Emerson said, "Wherever there is beauty, he will find a home."

The simple stone in the Concord cemetery was engraved with one word: *Henry*.

House:
An Epilogue

WHAT BECAME OF HENRY'S simple house at Walden Pond? The full story is interesting, if a bit perplexing. After Henry's occupancy, the ownership of the little house returned to Mr. Emerson, after which Hugh Whelan, Mr. Emerson's gardener, purchased it. Mr. Whelan moved the house a little farther from Walden Pond, dug a cellar, abandoned both, and moved somewhere else, leaving Henry's house tilting awkwardly into Hugh Whelan's cellar.

The house was later purchased by James Clark. Using an ox team, Clark moved it to his farm, where it was used to store grain. In 1868 the roof was lifted off and put over a pigpen. Seven years passed, during which time the floor and timbers were made into a shed at one end of Clark's barn. When this collapsed, the wood was rendered into patchwork for the barn itself.

However, as fate would have it, Clark's barn eventually became the property of Ralph Waldo Emerson's grandson. It was probably meant to be that way, since this was the solitary building that launched new ideas in American literature. No writer since Thoreau has covered more sacred, scientific, political, or natural ground. And his spiritual house, the symbol of American independence, lives on, roof and cellar, floor and walls, within the pages of *Walden*, one of the most influential books of our time.

Chronology

1817 Born July 12 in Concord, Massachusetts.

1823 Attends Miss Phoebe Wheeler's infant school.

1824 Attends the Center School.

1828 Attends Concord Academy.

1833 Enters Harvard College in Cambridge, Massachusetts.

1837 Graduates from Harvard, teaches for two weeks at the Center School. Meets and spends time with Ralph Waldo Emerson. Henry begins to write in his journal, a habit he develops and keeps for the rest of his life.

1838 Henry and his brother John open their own school in Concord.

1839 Meets the one love of his life, Ellen Sewall; travels on a homemade boat, the *Musketaquid*, down the Concord and Merrimack Rivers with John Thoreau.

1840 First publication, a poem and an essay, in *The Dial*. Proposes to Ellen Sewall and is refused.

1841 The school founded by Henry and John is closed owing to John's poor health. Henry moves into the Emerson house as a handyman.

1842 John Thoreau dies from tetanus poisoning. Waldo Emerson, the son of Ralph Waldo Emerson, dies as a result of scarlet fever. Henry meets Nathaniel Hawthorne for the first time. *The Dial* publishes eight of Henry's poems.

1843 Henry travels to Staten Island to tutor the children of William Emerson, brother of Ralph Waldo Emerson. Meets Horace Greeley, the influential editor of the *New York Tribune*. Returns to Concord in December.

1844 Sets the Concord woods on fire by mistake.

1845 Builds cabin at Walden Pond and moves in during the summer. During his two-year stay at Walden, Henry writes two books and fills many journals with his sharp observations of nature and humanity.

1846 Henry is jailed for not paying his poll tax.

1847 Leaves Walden Pond in September and moves back into the Emerson household.

1849 Publishes his essay about passive resistance in the *Aesthetic Papers*. The essay is first called "Resistance to Civil Government," but Henry later changes it to "Civil Disobedience." *A Week on the Concord and Merrimack Rivers* is published by James Monroe & Company. Visits Cape Cod with Ellery Channing.

1850   Travels to Canada with Ellery Channing.

1851   The Fugitive Slave Law is enacted. Henry is stirred to help runaway slaves escape to Canada. He speaks and writes against the institution of slavery.

1854   *Walden* is published by Ticknor & Fields.

1856   Henry meets Walt Whitman, the poet-author of *Leaves of Grass*, in Brooklyn. Whitman is one of the few people that Henry admires as a great writer and as a complete man.

1857   Henry meets John Brown, the great abolitionist. Travels to Maine with his Concord friend Edward Hoar.

1859   Henry's father, John Thoreau, dies. John Brown is arrested, tried, and executed for the insurrection at Harper's Ferry; Henry delivers a memorial speech in his honor.

1860   Henry becomes ill. The Civil War begins; Henry is sick all year.

1861   Travels to Minnesota in the hope that the drier air might revitalize him.

1862   Henry dies of complications from tuberculosis.

Glossary

ALGONQUIN. From the original word *Algonkin*, referring to the tribe of Native Americans living east of the present-day city of Ottawa, Canada. *Algonquian* is the family of languages spoken by this tribe as well as a broad range of tribes from northeastern to southeastern North America.

BROOK FARM. A community outside of Boston where transcendentalist George Ripley and his followers celebrated the oneness of nature: seeing God in all things found in the natural order of life. They raised their own vegetables and fruits and lived together in harmony. Fruitlands on Prospect Hill in Harvard was another community experiment. The founder was Bronson Alcott, a writer and friend of Ralph Waldo Emerson and father of three children, including Louisa May Alcott, author of *Little Women*. The community gave up eating meat and using oxen for plowing because these things killed and/or enslaved animals. They refused to wear wool because it was harvested from sheep. Their strict rules for living were so rigid that they left them unprepared for surviving a New England winter. The community failed the year it was founded.

DEPOT AGENT. A ticket issuer or collector; also a man who acted as a plainclothes security guard at railroad depots.

FUGITIVE SLAVE LAW. An 1851 law that imposed heavy penalties on people who helped any runaway slaves escape their masters.

HARPER'S FERRY. In 1859 John Brown, the militant abolitionist, raided the U.S. arsenal at Harper's Ferry, Virginia. With the guns that Brown hoped to capture, he would start a republic for free slaves somewhere in the Appalachian Mountains. Brown's capture and indictment resulted in his execution amid great protest from a variety of New England intellectuals.

HOD CARRIER. A man who carried hods at dockyards and depots and places of transport. A hod is a tray on a pole for carrying loads. It came to mean anyone carrying something heavy in colloquial situations, and it is still used today in the same way.

LYCEUM. A forum established in New England for the presentation of new ideas. Ralph Waldo Emerson led the way as a lecturer in this type of public format.

PENOBSCOT. American Indian tribe in central coastal Maine.

PICKEREL. A large freshwater fish often found in lakes.

PILLORY. A punishing device made of wood in which the head and hands are locked. Often identified with colonial times in America.

PLUMBAGO. Another name for graphite or pencil lead.

POLL TAX. A "flat tax"; a tax in which each citizen pays an equal amount of money to the government.

SALT FISH. Dried codfish packed, salted, and stored in boxes. Once cured, it did not spoil.

SANGAREE. From the Spanish word *sangre* (blood); a punch drink made with red wine; sangria.

SCARLET FEVER. A contagious disease characterized by sore throat, high fever, and a red rash. In some rare cases of "strep throat" the red rash of scarlet fever may be present. But it is easily treated with antibiotics.

SELECTMEN. Members of a governing body of a small New England community elected to enforce town laws.

SUMMER CELLAR. An underground storehouse lined with rock (to keep the space cool) that was used to store fruits and vegetables.

TETANUS. A disease caused by a cut or wound that becomes contaminated with tetanus bacteria. This infection affects the nervous system, causing the muscles of the body to spasm and grow rigid. Tetanus is also known as lockjaw because the muscles of the jaw eventually clamp shut and the patient can no longer open his or her mouth or swallow. Today children are immunized against tetanus, and as a result, it is a rare disease.

TRANSCENDENTALISM. A philosophical and spiritual movement in New England during the mid-nineteenth century headed by Ralph Waldo Emerson, Henry David Thoreau, Bronson Alcott, Ellery Channing, Margaret Fuller, and F. B. Sanborn. Transcendentalists believed that God is present in nature and within each human being. Therefore it wasn't necessary to attend church in order to be in the presence of the higher power. Transcendentalists also believed that people are born with an innate sense of right and wrong and can be left to themselves to act accordingly.

TRINITARIAN. A Protestant faith based on the idea that God is represented by three forms: God the Father, the Son, and the Holy Spirit. In transcendentalist thinking, God was singular, not one in three forms, but present within each individual.

UNDERGROUND RAILROAD. A system for getting runaway slaves from the South to the northern states or Canada, where they could live as free men and women. The "railroad" was largely made up of families who hid slaves along a designated route of escape. Thoreau hid slaves in his parents' house and personally took them to the railway station, bought their tickets, and got them safely onto trains to Canada.

UNITARIAN. A member of a religion founded by Ellery Channing's uncle, Reverend William Ellery Channing. The

Unitarians stressed individual freedom of belief, the free use of reason in religion, and a united world community.

WRIT. Past tense of "write"; an archaic or out-of-use word that was used as a noun, meaning a court order or summons.

Bibliography

Allen, F. H., ed. *Men of Concord.* Illustrated by N. C. Wyeth. Boston: Houghton Mifflin Co., 1936.

Canby, Henry Seidel. *Thoreau.* Boston: Houghton Mifflin Co., 1939.

Channing, W. E. *Thoreau: The Poet Naturalist.* New York: Biblo and Tannen, 1966.

Emerson, Edward. *Henry Thoreau as Remembered by a Young Friend.* Boston: Houghton Mifflin Co., 1917.

Epstein, Robert, and Sherry Phillips. *The Natural Man: Henry David Thoreau.* Wheaton, Ill.: Quest Books, 1978.

Harding, Walter. *The Days of Henry Thoreau.* Princeton, N.J.: Princeton University Press, 1962.

Kotz, Suzanne, and John Wawrzonek. *Walking.* Berkeley, Calif.: Nature Company, 1993.

Lawrence, Jerome, and Robert E. Lee. *The Night Thoreau Spent in Jail.* New York: Bantam, 1973.

Marble, Annie. *Thoreau: His Home, His Friends and Books.* New York: AMS Press, 1969.

McCarthy, Pat. *Henry David Thoreau: Writer, Thinker, Naturalist.* Berkeley Heights, N.J.: Enslow Publishers, 2003.

McKuen, Rod. *The Wind That Blows Is All Anybody Knows.* New York: Stanyan Books/Random House, 1970.

Murray, James G. *Henry David Thoreau.* New York: Washington Square Press, 1968.

Reef, Catherine. *Henry David Thoreau: A Neighbor to Nature.* Frederick, Md.: Henry Holt and Co., 1992.

Richardson, Robert. *Henry Thoreau: A Life of the Mind.* Berkeley: University of California Press, 1986.

Sanborn, F. B. *Hawthorne and His Friends: Reminiscence and Tribute.* Cedar Rapids, Iowa: Torch Press, 1908.

———. *Life of Henry David Thoreau.* Boston: Houghton Mifflin Co., 1917.

———. *The Personality of Thoreau.* Boston: Charles Goodspeed, 1901.

———. *Recollections of Seventy Years.* Vol. 2. Boston: Gorham Press, 1909.

Schnur, Steven, and Peter Fiore. *Henry David's House: Henry David Thoreau.* Watertown, Mass.: Charlesbridge Publishing, 2002.

Thoreau, Henry David. *Men of Concord.* Boston: Houghton Mifflin, 1936.

———. *Walden; Or, Life in the Woods.* Boston: Shambhala Publications, 2004.

———. *A Week on the Concord and Merrimack Rivers.* Edited by Carl F. Hovde. Princeton, N.J.: Princeton University Press, 1980.